RIDE INTO DANGER

Starbuck had no love for the brass buttons. Plus he had promised Melissa that his days of courting danger were over. But there was a troop of soldiers trapped by the marauding Utes and someone had to light out for help.

It was going to be one hell of a ride . . . through territory crawling with scalp-hungry Indians and murdering whites . . . where every blazing bullet had Lee Starbuck's name written on it!

RIDE INTO DANGER

Wayne D. Overholser

GUNSMOKE

This hardback edition 2002
by Chivers Press
by arrangement with
Golden West Literary Agency

ISBN 0 7540 8182 6

British Library Cataloguing in Publication Data available.

Printed and bound in Great Britain by
BOOKCRAFT, Midsomer Norton, Somerset

RIDE INTO DANGER

Chapter 1

LEE STARBUCK breathed an audible sigh of relief when he reached the White River Agency with the load of freight he had brought all the way from Rawlins, Wyoming. This was late September, 1879, his last trip, and more than once on the way south he had wished he wasn't making this one. He was lucky to be alive; he would be luckier still if he got back safely to his ranch on Bear River.

He had watched the ridges from the time he had left Bear Valley, particularly while he was coming down Coal Creek Canyon. He had not seen any Indians, but they were there, watching him. It was not a vagrant idea that drifts through a man's mind, but the certain knowledge that lies deep in his belly.

He'd had to guess at their intentions. If it was Nevero's band, they would shoot him out of the wagon seat. If it was Jack's, he wouldn't be harmed. Well, here he was at the Agency and he wasn't harmed, so it must have been Jack's.

Lee swung his horses between a storehouse and a new building that had not been roofed. All the buildings had been erected within the last year. The agent, Nathan Meeker, had moved the Agency downriver a dozen miles or so from the old site to this one in Powell Park. He had done a good job planning the physical layout of the Agency, Lee thought. It was unfortunate he was not as skillful in handling his personal relationship with the Utes.

Lee heard his name called as he stepped down from the seat. He turned to see Meeker striding toward him, his hand extended. The agent was relieved, Lee thought, to know that the road was still open, that the long-threatened outbreak of the Indians had not yet occurred.

"You look well, Mr. Starbuck," Meeker said as they shook hands. "I trust you had no difficulty on the road."

"None," Lee said.

1

"Arvilla and I would consider it a favor if you would have supper with us," Meeker said.

"Glad to," Lee said. "I remember Mrs. Meeker's cooking."

They walked together to the agent's house as soon as Meeker finished giving orders to some Agency employees concerning the storing of the goods Lee had brought. As they strode along the dusty street Lee glanced at Meeker, whose thoughts seemed far away, and he wondered if the agent realized how serious the trouble was.

Meeker was in his early sixties, a slender, straight-backed man with a strong face. He wore a frock coat, thus contriving to give an impression of dignity. On his earlier visits Lee had felt that Meeker appeared younger than he was, but the last weeks had aged him. The buoyancy and hopefulness that had once been a part of him were gone. He seldom smiled; and that, Lee thought, was too bad. He would have managed the Indians better if he had learned to laugh with them.

Mrs. Meeker greeted Lee warmly. "Supper will be ready soon," she said, and hurried back to the kitchen.

Meeker led Lee into a bedroom where there was water in a pitcher, a basin, and a clean towel. As he washed, he thought how one man's mistakes can bring disaster to other people, even sudden and violent death. He liked the Meekers as individuals, but they should have stayed in civilized Greeley east of the mountains. They didn't belong here, Nathan Meeker in particular, who was a visionary and lacked the practical sense that a man must have to deal with the Utes.

After supper Meeker took Lee to his office and told him how Johnson, the big medicine man who had been his best friend among the White River Utes, had come to his house and shouted a volley of words that Meeker couldn't follow, but he'd caught enough to gather that Johnson was furious because Meeker had ordered one of the Agency employees to plow some of his land.

"He accused me of sending lies to Washington," Meeker said. "I told him the trouble was he had too many ponies and he should kill some of them. This made him furious. He picked me up and pulled me outside and threw me against the hitching rail. The Indians who were watching laughed as if it was a fine show."

Meeker shook his head sadly. "He would have killed me if Arvilla hadn't screamed. Two of my men ran up and held Johnson. He walked off then. You see, Starbuck, it wasn't my body that he hurt so much. I thought he was my best friend. Now I know he is against me, too."

Lee nodded, thinking it was the worst kind of mistake for Meeker to tell Johnson he should kill some of his ponies. To Johnson this must have been a sort of blasphemy, and Meeker should have known it. He had made too many mistakes like this in the past, creating so much resentment among the Indians that they had asked for his removal.

"You've tried to change them too fast," Lee said.

"I know, I know." Meeker stood up and paced back and forth across the room. "But don't you see, Starbuck? We can't just sit and wait for social problems to solve themselves. If we are to progress, we have to force these things, and that is what I've been trying to do."

He stood at the window, his back to Lee. "I had so many plans for them," he said plaintively. "Not just farming, you understand. There is coal on the reservation. Logs to cut and saw into lumber. Fine pasture for cattle and sheep if they would only get rid of their ponies. A whole new life for them, a better life than any of the Ute tribes have ever known."

Here it was, Lee thought, a good man's dreams that had been doomed to failure from the beginning. The trouble went back to the fact that Meeker had never realized how basic was the change he had tried to force upon the Utes in his effort to move them from a pony culture to one based on farming and cattle raising.

Lee stood up. There was nothing for him to say. He felt as if he had just seen the curtain come down on the first act of a tragedy, the setting into motion of forces that could not be stopped, and must end in a great blood-letting.

Meeker faced Lee. "I came here with every intention of liking them and being kind to them," he said. "But since they haven't responded to decent human treatment, perhaps they will respond to force and brutality if the Army sees fit to deal with them that way."

Lee stared at the man, too stunned to say anything for a moment, and when he did his voice sounded strange to his ears. "You've sent for troops?"

"I had to," Meeker said. "You probably know John Steele, who has the mail contract between here and Rawlins. He spent the night of September tenth at the Agency and left the morning of the eleventh, so the message should have been wired out of Rawlins long before now."

3

· A wild anger that was close to madness took hold of Lee. He grabbed Meeker by the shoulders and shook him. "Do you know what you've done? Do you have the slightest idea?"

Meeker jerked free and backed away from him. "Of course I have. My wife and daughter Josie are here, along with Mrs. Price and her two children. I can't risk their lives. I don't have enough men to defend them if we have trouble. And another thing—the Indians are well armed. We can thank traders like Lucky Boman and Adam Simms for that."

"No, you don't know," Lee said. "You had a chance to keep the Indians peaceful, but you threw it away the minute you sent for troops. It's the one thing that will set them off."

"It was for our protection . . ."

"You won't be alive to need protection by the time the soldiers get here," Lee said furiously. "And do you know what will happen to me and the Frazer women who live next to me, and to everybody else on Bear River? They'll burn us out and kill us if they catch us. You might as well have—"

He stopped. There was no use to tell Meeker he was incompetent, that he had made every mistake he could in dealing with a primitive people like the Utes. Then, having made these mistakes, he had capped them with the biggest of all. He had sent for the Army.

"You'll hear the war drums tonight," Meeker said defensively. "You'll change your mind by morning."

Lee whirled and walked out of the room. No, there wasn't any use to tell Meeker what he thought. The man wouldn't understand. When the Utes killed him, he still wouldn't understand.

As Lee walked through the darkness to the storeroom office where he would sleep on a cot, he wondered if there was any way to countermand the order bringing the soldiers, but he decided it was too late.

He sat down on the edge of the cot, physically sick as he considered what Meeker had done. He thought about his boyhood on a Kansas ranch and about how he had hated the prairie and the wind and the heat and the dust; and how, after his folks had died from typhoid the summer he was fifteen, he had been forced to make his own living. He had no close kin, so he'd drifted into Colorado and kept on drifting, never finding a place where he wanted to stay and put his roots down until two years ago, when he had crossed the Continental Divide and had seen Bear Valley.

He had staked out a hundred sixty acres of choice bottom

land, and had built a log cabin, a corral, a barn, and other outbuildings he needed. Last summer and again this year he had hauled freight from Rawlins to the Agency to earn the cash money he needed to buy a herd of cattle when he could safely do so and not worry about a passing band of Utes stopping to butcher one or more of his best steers.

And now? He'd be lucky to stay alive through the coming weeks. And he'd be lucky not to get his place burned out. He thought of the Frazer women who lived downstream from him: Ma, who possessed the strength and tenacity of a man; Caroline, whom he once had thought he loved and now knew he did not; and Melissa, who had her mother's strength, but also possessed a tenderness he had never seen in Ma.

He pulled off his boots and lay down on the cot. Then the drums began to sound and there was no sleep for him. He lay there through the long, hideous hours, the air vibrating with the *thump-dum-dum, thump-dum-dum* of the drums. He kept his mind on Melissa and in that way tried to mute the sound.

Melissa had become a woman long before he'd realized it, and he wondered why he had been blind for so many months; but there was no doubt in his mind now. Melissa was the girl he wanted to marry when he returned to the Bear. Every word would have to be right when he asked her, but for some reason the right words eluded him.

Suppose a Ute war party swept down the Bear and murdered the Frazer women because of Meeker's blundering? He tried not to think of it, tried to keep the picture of Melissa's face alive in his mind, but another picture kept blotting it out—the picture of Melissa lying dead and scalped. He clenched his fists and felt the blood pound in his temples as he heard the pulsating sound of the drums and mentally cursed Nathan Meeker.

Chapter 2

SHORTLY AFTER sunup on Monday morning, September 22, 1879, Major Thomas Thornburgh led his command from

Rawlins south across the Wyoming plateau. The column stretched for two miles, from the Major up in front all the way back to the rear guard, Company E, Third Cavalry, under Captain Joe Lawson, who knew more about Indian fighting than the whole pack of them up in front. At least that was the carefully considered opinion of Private Billy Buckles.

Of course no one had asked Billy for an opinion. He wasn't surprised at that. After all, he was only twenty and he hadn't been in the Army very long. Still, he'd have had some answers if they had asked, because he knew a few things about the Utes.

"Funny business we're on," Billy said to Curly Joe Horn, who rode beside him. "We're going down here to save Father Meeker's hide, but the White River Agency is in Colorado, and Colorado ain't in the Department of the Platte, so what are we doing on this job?"

Curly Joe looked at him. Sometimes Curly Joe talked and sometimes he didn't. It wasn't that he couldn't talk. Curly Joe just didn't choose to talk most of the time. He was about thirty, Billy guessed, and he'd been in the Army ten years. If he talked at all about his past, it was about his experience as a soldier, with never a mention of anything that had happened before. Sometimes Billy wondered if Curly Joe had been born a private at the age of twenty.

"We're closest," Curly Joe said after a long pause, and turned his head to stare straight ahead at the column.

Billy shrugged and let it go. If Curly Joe didn't feel like talking, that was all there was to it. Billy did, but he didn't enjoy talking to himself. Well, he'd have to wait until Curly Joe was in a conversational mood, and that might not be until night.

Billy often wondered what Curly Joe thought about during his long periods of silence. Maybe about the Major and about Captain Scott Payne who rode beside him. It was natural enough for the men to think about their commanding officers and how they would stand up under pressure if there was a fight. Billy guessed that most of the men had their minds fixed on this very thing, but Curly Joe didn't think the way the other men did.

Well, maybe he was wondering who would die if there was a fight. He might tell Billy their names. He did things like that. It was enough to make a man wonder. Or he might even be thinking about nothing more profound than the dust that hung above the column and lay in a long wake behind it and covered men and horses with a gray coat and got into every opening of a man's hide, even into his mouth, where it gritted between his teeth and sent shivers up and down his spine.

Billy shrugged, deciding that trying to guess what Curly Joe Horn was thinking about was a poor project for any man. Besides, he had a few people to think about himself. Lee Starbuck, for instance. Billy had worked for Lee on his ranch last summer, looking after the horses and grubbing sagebrush while Lee was hauling freight between Rawlins and the Agency.

When Lee returned to the ranch, he would tell Billy about the trip and the Indians he had seen, such as Douglas, the old chief, and Jack, who had a bigger following than Douglas, and Colorow, the fat one who claimed he was a chief, too.

And Lee would talk about the Meekers, Nathan and his wife Arvilla and their twenty-year-old daughter Josie, and he'd always wind up saying something like, "I never knew a man who wanted to do right as much as Meeker, or one who makes bigger mistakes. He just don't have no give, and you don't get along with a man like Jack unless you know how and when to give."

Billy wished Thornburgh knew that about both Meeker and Jack, but the chances were he didn't. Private Billy Buckles would get his butt kicked right out of Company E if he rode up to the Major and said, "I know some things you ought to know about the Indian agent we're coming down here to save, and about Jack and the other chiefs." No, you didn't get anything in the Army but trouble if you started giving advice to your commanding officer.

Billy would have felt better, too, if Lee Starbuck were guiding Thornburgh's command instead of Joe Rankin, who was riding somewhere out on the flank as if he thought they'd find Indians before they reached the Colorado line. Not that there was anything wrong with Rankin. It was just that Starbuck lived here and he knew both the country and the Indians.

Well, there *was* something wrong with Rankin, now that he thought about it, wrong by Billy Buckles's standards anyway. Rankin talked too loud, he laughed too loud, and he was just a little too sure of himself. Besides, he wore a suit of white buckskin, and that struck Billy as being all wrong.

Maybe the trouble was that Billy measured the local people

by Lee Starbuck, and Lee set a hard standard to come up to. He was honest, he'd tell you the truth even if it hurt like hell, and he was competent. More than that, he respected the Utes. He didn't particularly like them, but he knew they were not the degenerate tribe some people said they were. They'd fight if they were pushed far enough, and Meeker had been doing a lot of pushing.

He might be wrong about Rankin, Billy told himself. He didn't really know the man, although he'd seen him a number of times around Rawlins, where he ran a livery stable. It was just that he knew Lee Starbuck well, and Lee lived closer to the reservation than Rankin did.

Billy respected anyone who lived in Bear Valley. If war came, the settlers would be cleaned out and their buildings burned all the way up to Steamboat Springs, and maybe even on over the range into North Park and Middle Park. Only one kind of people would stick in the face of that kind of danger—men like Lee Starbuck and women like the Frazers, Ma and Caroline and Melissa. His heart picked up momentum as he thought about Melissa. If he'd just had a little more time with her, maybe he'd have worked up nerve enough to have told her he loved her.

The column threw off at noon, the men eating cold bacon sandwiches. Curly Joe was still silent, his gaze on Joe Rankin, who was riding in from the east. He was probably going to report to Major Thornburgh that he hadn't seen any evidence of hostilities; and that, Billy thought in disgust, was something he could have told the Major without riding out there to hellangone.

Rankin rode toward the front of the column, nodding to some of the men he knew and waving to others. When he reached Billy and Curly Joe and Amen Brown, the trooper who rode in front of Billy, he pulled up and said, motioning toward Billy, "Little man, that's a hell of a big horse you're riding. It's a long ways to the ground from the saddle."

Billy was the smallest man in the company, a fact that was a sore point with him and one that had been the cause of more fights than he could remember. Now he lunged toward the guide, his hands instinctively closing into fists. He yelled, "Get off that horse, Rankin. I'll show you . . ."

Rankin rode on, laughing loudly. Amen Brown shouted, "Come back here, you loud-mouthed . . ."

But Rankin didn't come back. Curly Joe said gently, "The fears of men are many."

Billy looked at him, his anger still boiling. He didn't have the slightest idea what Curly Joe was talking about, but he knew from experience that the trooper had an irritating way of talking about something that was completely irrelevant to the subject at hand.

"That's right," Amen Brown said.

"I guess so, Joe," Billy agreed.

He wondered where the man had read it. Curly Joe read a great deal, mostly the Bible and classics that Billy didn't understand. He was always quoting something or voicing a profound idea of his own, and unless he mentioned who he was quoting, Billy was never sure whether the thought was original or not.

"Man is afraid to be born when he is being carried in his mother's womb," Curly Joe said. "After that he's afraid to live, and he's more afraid to die. He's afraid for himself and his family and his friends. He's afraid of the future because it's hidden from his eyes by a fog so thick he cannot see through it. That is a blessing, but he doesn't know it. If he could see the future, he would be more afraid than ever."

Sergeant Pat O'Brien's commanding voice rolled back along the line, "Prepare to mount. . . . Mount."

Again the column rolled south, dust rising in a suffocating cloud and slowly spreading out and settling on the sagebrush. Billy considered what Curly Joe had said concerning fear. He hadn't thought about it that way before, which wasn't unusual with the things Curly Joe said.

Billy stared at the hump the Colorado mountains made against the sky, and wondered what would happen when they reached Ute country. Curly Joe was right about one thing. It was lucky Billy didn't know what was going to happen, or he wouldn't be able to endure the next few days.

When the company had been ordered out of Fort Steele, neither Major Thornburgh nor Captain Lawson nor anyone else had come around and said exactly what was ahead. Maybe no one knew, but there had been plenty of talk, most of it wild and all of it confused. Then at Rawlins they'd met two companies from Fort D. A. Russell and there had been more talk, just as confused and wild as the earlier talk had been.

But Billy wasn't sure that had anything to do with what

Curly Joe had said. He was still thinking about it when Curly Joe broke his silence: "Emerson said, 'We are afraid of truth, afraid of fortune, afraid of death, and afraid of each other.' Right now we're afraid of the Utes, and we should be. More than that, everybody at White River Agency has cause to be afraid. I've got a feeling about it." Curly Joe turned his head to look at Billy. "You afraid, boy?"

Billy's gaze met Curly Joe's. Whenever the man had a premonition, he talked of a feeling. Billy had heard him mention enough of them that had worked out in one way or another to form a healthy respect for any prophesies he made.

A prickle worked along Billy's spine and settled between his shoulder blades. He hadn't been afraid, or hadn't thought he was. He had never been in action, and Curly Joe had. In fact, many of the men in Thornburgh's command had smelled powdersmoke, most of it from Sioux rifles, and that was probably the reason some of them took the Utes as lightly as they did.

Now, looking at Curly Joe's dark, weathered face, it seemed to Billy that he was staring at the face of destiny. Curly Joe claimed that God had your number racked up right beside Him in Heaven, and if he reached out and flipped it over, you were a goner.

"I guess I am afraid," Billy admitted, and was aware that the prickle had slid along his spine again.

"Good. That's an honest answer." Curly Joe stared at the back of the trooper in front of him. "We spend all of our lives marching down the halls of our fears. The craven coward cringes and trembles and perhaps tries to escape by running, but the brave man controls his fears. When the time comes, that is what you will do, and the inches that God gave you has nothing to do with it."

That was the end of the conversation. Billy could tell it by the way Curly Joe stared ahead, by the frowning lines in his forehead, by the dark and brooding expression in his eyes and the tightness of his lips. At such a time Billy could talk for ten minutes about the weather or his horse or Major Thornburgh or anything else, but Curly Joe wouldn't hear a word he said. But now Billy knew what Curly Joe had been getting at in his devious way. He was trying to tell Billy that he'd better quit worrying about how small he was, that a little man can be just as brave as a big one when the chips are down.

10

Billy thought about that and knew he had to believe it. If he really believed it, he could quit trying to prove how good a man he was by fighting everyone who made a remark about his size. He did himself more harm by wanting to fight all the time than he would by swallowing his pride and letting some of the remarks go. At least that was what Melissa used to tell him.

This turned his thoughts to the Frazer women. There was Ma, so stubborn she was determined to stay on Bear River next to Lee Starbuck's ranch, even though her husband had been murdered by a renegade band of Utes more than a year ago. There was Caroline, who was about Billy's age, green-eyed, with a doll-like perfection of features and a hip-swaying walk that made it rough for a man to stand still and watch her. And then there was Melissa, tall and long-legged and slim-bodied, with brown eyes and hair so dark it was almost black.

In Billy's eyes Caroline was a flirt, and worse—a bitchy woman who delighted in arousing a man and then laughing in his face; but Melissa was so different it was hard to believe they were sisters. Billy had been in love with her from the first week he'd worked for Lee Starbuck and she had come to Lee's place to cook Sunday dinner for him.

But Billy knew Melissa didn't love him. Oh, he had never come right out and asked her how she felt, but he knew. For one thing, she couldn't see any man but Lee, and Lee seemed to think she was still a girl. Besides, Billy had nothing to offer her, so what was the point of telling her how he felt?

On they rode, south across the Wyoming plateau toward the Ute country. Billy, for want of anything else as pleasant to think about, kept his mind on Melissa and wondered if the command would make a night camp on the Bear, and if it did, could he get permission from Captain Lawson to go to see her? He'd ask, he told himself. The old man couldn't any more than say no.

Chapter 3

THORNBURGH'S COMMAND moved forward steadily. The Wyoming plateau was monotonous with the dusty gray of the sage and the green-gray of rabbit brush. On Tuesday afternoon they reached the valley of the Little Snake, a different world from the wind-swept region they had crossed, a colorful world where the aspens and scrub oak and serviceberry brush had been painted bright yellow and scarlet by a lavish nature.

The scene was not new to Private Billy Buckles, for he had looked at similar beauty when he had worked for Lee Starbuck the year before in Bear Valley. For some reason that wasn't clear to Billy, Curly Joe Horn became tremendously excited as he took in the scene before him.

"Beautiful," Curly Joe said. "Purely beautiful. Did you ever see anything like it, Billy?"

"Yeah," Billy said indifferently. "It's better the farther south you go."

"Impossible," Curly Joe said. "It couldn't be. This is exactly like Heaven. I've had a few glimpses of it, and the one thing that always impresses me is the brightness of the color. Let him who has eyes see."

"I've got eyes, and all I'm looking at right now is some scrub oak," Billy said. "Now tell me just when you had a look at Heaven, and was there any scrub oak in sight? Or maybe some prickly pear?"·

The conversation stopped right there. Curly Joe had nothing more to say, not even later when the column made camp and Major Thornburgh and Lieutenant Sam Cherry rode off up the river to visit the old mountain man, Jim Baker, who lived there with his squaws. When twilight flowed across the valley and the cook fires became twitching eyes in the darkness, Curly Joe sat by himself staring into the flames, a strange, withdrawn man who seemed to have one foot in this world and the other in a world Billy Buckles had never seen.

12

Amen Brown, who shared the cook fire, looked at Billy and shook his head. "He's the damnedest man I ever seen," he said in a low tone.

"Right now he wouldn't hear what you said if you thundered in his ear," Billy told Brown. "He gets that way sometimes. Kind of like he pulls down curtains all around him so he can be alone."

Brown nodded. "I've seen him this way before, but he's never like that when there's something to be done. I mean, if I was betting my last blue chip and I had my druthers about who I had beside me, I'd take Curly Joe every time."

"I would, too," Billy said. "But he's a queer one all the same. I've heard Sergeant O'Brien threaten to kick him clean out of Company E."

Brown laughed silently, his shoulders shaking. "The Sergeant has threatened to kick him out of the whole United States Army, but he won't. Curly Joe is a better soldier than O'Brien will ever be."

Brown scratched a bearded cheek, then he went on. "God moves in mysterious ways. It ain't given us to understand everything that happens, but I know He's got a certain use for all of us. I think He's given Curly Joe second sight, and we'd better pay attention to everything he says."

Billy didn't believe that Curly Joe had second sight any more than the next man. The Sergeant, for instance, seemed to have second sight when some of the Company E boys had a little devilment afoot; but Billy never argued with Amen Brown, who could always rake up enough Bible quotations to snow a man under. That gave Billy two choices, both of them bad. He could admit he was wrong, or say the Bible was wrong. Either way Brown had him.

The scout, Joe Rankin, was moving from fire to fire and talking in his usual loud voice about how the Utes didn't have the get-up and go of the Sioux or Cheyennes, and there wouldn't be any trouble. Sure, they were tricky, but they just weren't fighters. The whole column could march right over Yellow Jacket Pass and camp beside Agent Meeker's house and there wouldn't be a shot fired. And if there was a man in the outfit who was worried about his hide getting perforated by a bullet or a Ute arrow, he'd best just forget it.

Rankin was standing at the next fire holding forth with his usual tone and words. Billy said to Amen Brown, "If I had me a sharp enough knife, I'd stick it into that wind bag and let the air out and we'd be blown clean down to the Bear."

Amen Brown laughed. The idea of Billy Buckles taking on the big scout was about as realistic as a half-pint tying into a full gallon. "Don't do it," Brown warned. "That's too long a trip by air."

"Here he comes," Billy muttered. "I wonder if the Major sent him around to pump some bravery into us."

"No," Brown said. "Thornburgh wouldn't do that."

Rankin stepped close to the fire and glanced at Curly Joe on the other side, then at Billy and Amen Brown, and said, "Well, boys, there's been some talk about us having a fight with the Utes, but the way I see it—"

"Don't waste your misdirected wind and unreliable information on us," Curly Joe said as he stood up and pinned his gaze on the scout's face. "There will be a fight."

Rankin felt insulted, and at the same time he was puzzled. He stood motionless for a moment, an impressive figure in his buckskins, his eyes on Curly Joe. The soldiers always listened to him as if his words were gospel, so for a Private to stand up and say what Curly Joe had just said was not only disrespectful, but close to being sacrilege.

"He's right," Billy said quickly. "I lived down here last summer and I saw several of the chiefs. I can tell you that Nevero would cut your throat on a dark night if he had half a chance. And Colorow . . ."

"A fat coward," Rankin scoffed. "A thief and a coward."

Curly Joe raised a hand. "The Book of Jeremiah says, 'He that fleeth from the fear shall fall into the pit; and he that getteth up out of the pit shall be taken in the snare.' "

Curly Joe sat down and, leaning forward, took off his hat and wiped his forehead. Rankin stared at him and cursed in a low tone. Curly Joe was completely bald, and his head was shiny bright in the firelight, except for an area that was hideously scarred.

"He's been scalped," Rankin said in awe. "Where did it happen, man?"

But Curly Joe now had both feet in the other world and did not hear the question. Billy dug an elbow into Rankin's ribs. "He don't hear nothing when he gets like that. He's never told any of us, so he sure as hell ain't gonna tell you."

Rankin walked off as if he were dazed. Amen Brown gave a quiet laugh and said, "You know, Billy, I ain't real sure Curly Joe gets as far off when he's in one of them fits as he wants us to think."

14

"I've thought the same thing more'n once," Billy said. "I never felt sure about it, but then I don't understand half of what he says. Like talking to Rankin that way. What did he mean by quoting Jeremiah?"

"It's my guess that Rankin is more afraid than he wants anybody to realize, and Curly Joe knew it," Brown answered, "so he was telling Rankin that he's going to fall into a pit if he ain't careful."

Later that night Billy thought about it as he stood guard in the darkness. He told himself that there was nothing to worry about here on the Little Snake. They were still a long ways from Ute country; and although some of the bands wandered farther from the reservation than this, it was not likely they would be roving around now. After all, the White River Utes were a small tribe, and there were 153 soldiers and 25 civilians camped along the Little Snake.

No, a Ute brave wasn't likely to be here, ready to spring out of the darkness and slip a knife blade between a man's shoulder blades. But tomorrow night, or the next night, or whenever the column crossed the Bear, a Ute warrior might be sneaking through the sagebrush, and he, Private Billy Buckles of Company E, Third Cavalry, could die without ever having seen Melissa Frazer again.

He had to see Melissa, he told himself. He had to tell her he loved her and ask her to wait until he was out of the Army and could make a home for her; he had to tell her that he had carried the picture of her face in his mind all year since he had left the Bear and had never even as much as looked at another girl in the time since he had seen her. It would be only a small lie, because the girls he had visited in Rawlins were professionals and didn't count.

He'd ask to leave the company for a few hours, he decided. He remembered that he'd told himself the same thing before, but he hadn't said a word to Captain Lawson. He guessed he was afraid of the old man. Maybe it would be smarter to ask Sergeant O'Brien.

That was what he did in the morning, and immediately he regretted it. O'Brien threw back his beefy shoulders and twisted the points of his red mustache between thumbs and forefingers as he considered Billy's statement that he wanted permission to ride upstream to see Melissa Frazer when they reached the Bear, and that he'd rejoin Company E in a few hours. It was very important, he said.

"Is it, now?" O'Brien said softly, then he opened his big mouth and bellowed, "By God, who do you think you are, General Sherman's favorite nephew?"

O'Brien wheeled and strode off. Billy stared at his broad back, not realizing until that moment how much he hated the tough sergeant. Later O'Brien's commanding tone ran back along the line, "Prepare to mount . . . . Mount!"

He hated the big mick, all right, and he wondered how and why he'd ever got into the Army to be kicked around by a man like Pat O'Brien. But there had to be a way to get around him.

He heard Curly Joe Horn's question: "Did you ever see a finer morning, Billy?" Then came Captain Lawson's order: "Column of twos . . . walk . . . ho." Captain Lawson, Billy decided, was the man to go to. All he needed was the right excuse, but wanting to see Melissa wasn't it.

He centered his mind on the problem during the climb over the divide to Fortification Creek, but he couldn't free his thoughts from Melissa long enough to think of any solution. If he just took off he'd be a deserter, and probably would get shot. But there had to be a way, he told himself, there just had to be.

Chapter 4

LEE STARBUCK climbed out of Coal Creek Canyon and topped Yellow Jacket Pass before he became aware that two Indians were following him. From a distance he could not recognize them. He kept watching, and now and then he had a good view of both of them when they rode out of the brush into the open, but still he was not able to identify them.

He camped that evening on Milk Creek, knowing there was no use to make a run for it. Even with an empty wagon, they would catch him if he tried it. Such a show of fear would make death certain, whereas he felt that at the moment they had no hostile intent.

He took care of his horses and made a fire and cooked supper, keeping his Winchester handy. He felt sure that the

Indians were not far away. Probably they were watching him from the cedars, but he still wasn't worried. Most Utes were good shots, and if they had wanted to kill him they could have done it any time during the last four or five hours.

He was reasonably sure that there would be no real violence until the soldiers came. In the past a few white men had been murdered by the Utes, but usually it had been off the reservation and had been done by a small band of renegade braves, probably with some of Lucky Boman's rotgut whisky in them. This was the way it had been with Pa Frazer, who had been chopping wood on the north bank of the river. None of the Utes had been punished. Neither had Boman, although it was Lee's opinion that Boman was more guilty than the Ute who had pulled the trigger.

The sun was down and the light was fading fast when the two Indians who had been following Lee rode into camp. One was the subchief Nevero, squat and heavy-faced, as were most Utes; the other was Jack, who was as tall and lithe as an Arapaho and did not look like his people.

Jack was about forty, well built, with good shoulders and a strong chin. He carried a Henry rifle in his right hand. He wore his hair in two long braids down his back. Having been raised by a Mormon family, he spoke better English than the average Ute. As usual, he was wearing the clothes that had been issued to him when he had scouted for General Crook: a cowboy hat and boots, buckskin pants, and a fringed jacket. All of these showed a good deal of wear, and Lee remembered he had not seen Jack wearing anything else since he had returned from the Sioux campaign.

Nevero did not resemble Jack in any way, even in his clothing. He wore a blue shirt, overalls, and a rolled-up U.S.I.D. blanket around his waist. A faded derby was perched on the top of his big head. He too carried a Henry rifle. Lee knew that he was treacherous, and he would have been worried if Jack had not been there.

Both Indians stayed on their horses for a time, their moccasin-clad feet in the rope stirrups. Finally Nevero extended his hand and said, "How."

Lee shook hands. He said, "How," and motioned toward the fire. "Want a cup of coffee?"

Nevero dismounted and said, "Belly heap empty." Jack stepped down and held out his hand. "How," he said.

Lee shook hands with him and asked, "Coffee, Jack?"

The chief nodded. "Good."

17

Both Indians squatted by the fire while Lee poured the coffee into tin cups and handed it to them. Lee lighted a cigar, and when the Indians finished their coffee he handed cigars to them.

Nevero picked up a burning stick and held the flame to his cigar. When he had it going he asked, "What you do here?"

Nevero knew as well as Lee did. The subchief had seen him on the road many times both last summer and this. He was irritated by the question, but it would not do to show his feelings. He said, "I delivered a load of freight at the Agency. I'm on my way home now. This is my last trip."

"What haul?" Nevero asked.

"Flour, sugar, molasses, coffee, blankets, and condensed milk."

"Rifles?"

"No rifles, no ammunition, and no revolvers," Lee said. "I guess there was a sewing machine."

Jack had been staring directly at Lee all this time, his dark eyes expressionless. Now he said, "We follow you since noon. You 'fraid?"

Lee shook his head. "Why should I be afraid? We're friends. I've been freighting stuff for your people all summer, stuff you didn't get before Agent Meeker came."

"Meeker no good." Nevero jerked the cigar out of his mouth and spat into the fire. "Meeker God damn."

Lee remained silent, watching Jack. Nevero had said exactly what Lee had expected him to say, but it wasn't important. On the other hand, what Jack said and thought was of the greatest importance. For several years his influence had steadily increased with the White River Utes until more than a hundred lodges supported him now. Although the government recognized Douglas, the old one, as chief, his power had declined until he had only about twenty lodges.

The hard truth was that it was Jack who would decide the question of war or peace, and not Douglas, or the noisy ones like Nevero and Colorow. So the minutes passed, Lee smoking and waiting for Jack to speak. He knew it would be useless and perhaps dangerous to hurry him.

Finally Jack said, "Meeker send for soldiers. Utes no 'fraid. Fort Steele soldiers women. Utes fight heap big."

"You won't get anywhere fighting," Lee said. "If you whip the first bunch they send, more will come. You've seen them. You know what I'm saying is true."

"Utes tell Meeker to stop plow," Jack went on, ignoring what Lee had said. "Meeker say Utes work. Utes no like work. Utes hunt. No like school. No go."

"School." Nevero spat into the fire again. "God damn."

Jack looked directly at Lee. "Meeker say soldiers bring chains for Utes. He say soldiers send us to Florida. You tell soldiers Utes fight like hell. Utes no go to Florida. Soldiers stay away. No trouble."

That was what he had come to say, Lee thought as he watched Jack walk to his pony. Nevero threw his cigar stub into the fire. "Meeker God damn," he said, and followed Jack to the ponies.

"You're bound to lose if you fight," Lee said. "Maybe you'll even lose your reservation." He paused, and added, "Besides, Ouray wouldn't like it."

Both men whirled to face him and he realized belatedly that he had said the wrong thing. Ouray lived near the Los Piños Agency on the Uncompahgre far to the south, on the other side of the Grand. Although the government considered him the head of the Ute nation, he had very little authority on White River, where many of the chiefs and subchiefs actually hated him.

Nevero swung his rifle to cover Lee. "Ouray 'Pache papoose. Son of a bitch."

"Point that rifle the other way," Lee said sharply. "I'm not Ouray."

Jack spoke in Ute to Nevero, who grumbled something in reply, then both men mounted. Jack sat motionless for a moment, his black eyes inscrutable. Finally he said, "You friend. You tell soldiers Utes fight. Utes get guns from Boman and Simms. Utes kill."

Then they rode away, disappearing a moment later in the darkness. Lee kicked out his fire and went to bed, but not to sleep. He stared at the sky and thought there was nothing he or anyone else could do to avert tragedy. Jack's and Nevero's visit had been the beginning of the second act.

It would be useless, Lee knew, to saddle his horse when he reached the Bear and ride to Fort Steele and tell Major Thornburgh what Jack had said, although this was what Jack expected him to do. Thornburgh was very likely on his way south now; but whether he was or not, he would do what he was ordered to do, not what Lee Starbuck advised.

All Utes hated the soldiers because they feared them. Lee knew this, but he had not known how much the Utes were afraid of being sent to Florida in chains. If Meeker had made this threat to keep them in line, he had been as foolish as when he had sent for the soldiers. He should have known, as Lee did, that the Utes would rather die in battle here in this land that was their ancestral home than to be sent in chains to Florida, where they would die of malaria.

Tonight Jack had been Lee's friend, but after the first shot was fired, the Utes would have no white friends on either the White River or the Bear. And because he could not stand the thought of Melissa being captured or murdered by the Utes, he rose before dawn, harnessed his horses, and drove north through the darkness.

Ma Frazer was the most stubborn woman he had ever known, but he had to convince her that she must take the girls and go to Steamboat Springs until the trouble was over. He wasn't at all sure that he could. He doubted that anyone had ever changed Ma Frazer's mind once she had made a decision.

The only other course he could think of was to marry Melissa in Steamboat Springs and remain there with her until it was safe to return to his ranch. But what he wanted to do was stay on the ranch and protect his buildings.

The sun rose and the day turned warm. With the passage of the hours, the miles between him and the Bear were steadily cut down, but still he could think of no adequate answer to the problem.

Chapter 5

THE SUN, blood-red, was a full circle above the western hills when Lee reached the Bear. The river was low enough for him to ford it just below his barn, and when he pulled around the barn and saw the cabin he stopped to stare at it in surprise. A column of smoke rose straight up from the chimney into the still evening air.

He swung to the ground just as Melissa stepped through the doorway. For a moment they stared at each other, then she called, "Lee, I've been worried."

He ran to her across the grass, forgetting the pretty words he had thought of saying and, taking her in his arms, kissed her long and hard. When he let her go, she whispered breathlessly, "Oh, why haven't you ever done that before?"

"Will you marry me, Melissa?" he asked. "Tomorrow, or day after tomorrow, if we can find a preacher in Steamboat Springs?"

"Of course I'll marry you." She looked at him, her lips trembling, and for a moment he thought she was going to cry, then she said, "What has happened that you're asking me just now? This way. I mean, you've known me for two years, and it always seemed that Caroline was between us."

"She was at first," he said, "but I haven't seen her or even wanted to see her for a long time."

"But why ask me just now?" Melissa asked again. "You acted as if you might not see me again."

He kept his gaze on her for a long moment without answering. This tall, slender girl with brown eyes and dark, dark hair lacked Caroline's doll-like perfection of features, but she was attractive. Her mouth was sweetly shaped, her cheeks were bright with color. She carried herself proudly, her shoulders back, her breasts high; and now, seeing her as he did, he wondered if she had become a woman overnight —or had he simply failed to see her as she was?

"I love you, Melissa," he said slowly. "It wasn't that I just discovered it when I saw you come out of the cabin. I wanted to wait until I had things a little better for you. Caroline called my cabin a boar's nest. Maybe it is, but I guess we could live in it. When I was at the Agency I heard the Ute war drums and Meeker said he'd sent for troops. Well, it seems foolish to wait. We'd be wasting time."

He took a long breath, then he blurted, "I've got to get you out of here, Melissa. I just couldn't stand it when I thought about the Utes coming and killing you—or capturing you, which would be even worse."

"I'm glad," she said. She kissed him and turned toward the cabin. "Supper's almost ready. I didn't know when you'd be back, so I started it early."

He unhooked the horses and took care of them, then he hurried into the cabin, thinking it was a pleasure to come home to a hot supper. He poured water from a bucket into a basin and washed, then picked up a comb and ran it through his brown hair, which he kept clipped short, so that it stood straight up above his forehead. He used the comb on his bristly, downslanting mustache that was more red than brown, and after that he sat down at the table.

He was twenty-nine, tall and hard-muscled, a man who had found and claimed here on the north bank of the Bear the piece of land he wanted. Here were his dreams, his ambitions; he would grow with the country, once the Indian trouble was settled, for then the people would come.

He had been one of the first to settle on the Bear and he'd had his choice of the land, but it had been at the risk of his life. That was why the mistakes Meeker had made and the mistakes the Army would make—it seemed to him that the Army always made mistakes—were so important to him and the Frazers and the other settlers.

Time and sweat and countless hours of labor had gone into building his log cabin and barn and sheds; he had a good deal of money invested in his horses, too. If war came and he was wiped out, he would have to start all over again.

He watched Melissa move briskly as she brought food to the table from the stove: venison steaks, boiled potatoes, gravy, biscuits and honey, and coffee. He had hoped to give her so much more than this crude cabin and equally crude furniture, but in a week there might not even be this much.

She dropped onto a bench across the table from him. For a moment he sat motionless, looking at her as a wave of emotion washed over him. For a moment he could not speak. She asked, "Aren't you hungry? Or doesn't my cooking—"

"You're the best cook in the world," he said. "I was thinking it isn't right for you to have to come here and keep house in a place like this. If they burn us out, we'll be lucky to find a tent to live in this winter. I wanted—"

"Oh, honey," she interrupted. She rose and came around the table and kissed him. "I'm not Caroline, and I don't think your cabin is a boar's nest. This is all I want or need. I want you for a husband. I want you for the father of my children. Now you go ahead and eat your supper."

Later, while she was doing the dishes, he sat and smoked and told her of his talk with Meeker and of the visit Jack and Nevero had made him. When he had finished, she said, "Ma wants you to come and see her as soon as you can. Caroline has been gone all day. Maybe we never told you, but Nevero has stopped several times at our place. He's tried to get Caroline to go with him and be one of his wives. She just laughs at him. Once Ma picked up a gun and ran him off. She thinks Nevero has Caroline."

"I suppose she's been out riding again," Lee said angrily. "Hasn't she got any sense? She knows what the situation is. So does your ma."

Melissa turned back to the dishpan. "They know, but Caroline is Caroline. She's always done what she pleased. She hates it here. She's ding-donged at Ma to move back across the mountains ever since Pa was killed. Ma's always done what Caroline wanted except for this."

She carried the dishpan to the back door and emptied it, and when she came back, her lips trembling, she said, "I don't think Nevero has her, Lee."

He nodded, knowing what Melissa meant. The chances were Caroline was with Lucky Boman. He stood up and paced around the room, pulling hard on his pipe. His thoughts went back to the previous summer when he had thought he loved Caroline and wanted to marry her, but even then she had showed she preferred Boman's company to his. She had hurt him in a way no other woman ever had. Now, looking back, he thought she had enjoyed doing it.

He had been blind for a long time, and her mother still was, believing the lies Caroline told her and not once suspecting she was seeing Boman. Ma Frazer had told the trader she'd shoot him if he showed up around their place and she had forbidden Caroline to see him or speak to him. Because Ma trusted the girl, it had been easy to fool her, and neither Lee nor Melissa had told Ma the truth because they knew she wouldn't believe them.

Lee came to stand beside Melissa. "What does she see in Boman?"

Melissa finished drying the dishes and hung up the cloth. She said, "You want to walk home with me? I promised Ma I'd fetch you if you didn't get in too late."

"Sure I'll walk home with you." He caught Melissa's arms. "What does she see in Boman?" he said again. "I know him, and I know Adam Simms. They both deserve to hang. She must know what kind of a man he is."

She looked at him and shook her head. "I don't know what she sees in him."

"What does your ma want to talk to me about?"

"I'll wait and let her tell you."

She walked out of the cabin into the twilight. He caught up with her and turned downstream toward the Frazer place, her long legs matching his stride. The smell of fall was in the air, and now that the sun was down, the wind was sharp with the portent of winter. He reached out and took Melissa's hand and held it as they walked. More than anyone else, she had been hurt by Caroline and she could not talk about her sister without being bitter.

"Would it have helped if I'd told you before that I love you?" he asked.

She gave him a small smile. "Yes, Lee. It would have helped."

"I thought you knew how I felt," he said. "I mean, I've asked you to go with me to the dances in Steamboat Springs whenever I was home. I've tried to be with you as much as I could."

She squeezed his hand. "That helped, Lee. It's just that—well, I guess a woman wants to be told she's loved. Besides, I was afraid you wouldn't realize I was different from Caroline."

"I knew," he said quickly. "If it wasn't for Ma, I'd let her stay right where she is. I'll fetch her back if that's what Ma wants, and then I think I'll tell her where Caroline was. She can call me a liar if she wants to, but this has gone so far it's ridiculous."

"It's more than ridiculous. It's crazy."

They reached the Frazer house and went in. Melissa said, "I'll light a lamp and go find Ma. You sit down."

After Melissa had gone out through the back, Lee glanced around and was amazed, as he always was, by what the Frazer women had done with the interior of a rude log cabin. The dirt floor was covered with elk and deer hides. The walls were whitewashed. A stone fireplace took up nearly all of one wall. Pa Frazer, who had been a good fireplace man, had hauled rocks from the river and built the biggest and best-drawing fireplace anywhere on the Bear.

The women had converted two soap boxes into stools, covering each with cushions of bright print, pleating the material all the way down to the floor, so that the stools were not only comfortable but added to the attractiveness of the room.

The window curtains, tied back by red ribbons, were white. A table in the middle of the room was covered by a red and black cloth with lace around the edge. This was largely Caroline's work; it was what she liked to do and apparently Ma had always let her do what she wanted, while she made Melissa work in the field.

The lace that Caroline had crocheted for the table spread had taken hours of her time. She had a right to call his cabin a boar's nest, Lee thought; but all he could think of now was that he had been lucky he hadn't married her. Melissa, he knew, was right for him, and he hoped he would be right for her.

Ma Frazer came in through the back door, calling out in her big voice, "I'm glad you're back, Lee. I hear the Utes are getting ornerier every day."

"They're more than ornery," he said. "They're downright mean. I want you and the girls to start for Steamboat Springs in the morning and stay there till things cool off."

She looked at him as if he had gone crazy. She was a big-boned woman with a square jaw; her brown hair had turned white since her husband's death. She could handle an axe or a plow as well as a man, and seemed to enjoy it. Lee suspected she had spoiled Caroline because she saw in the older girl the qualities she knew she herself completely lacked.

"I won't do no such thing and you know it, Lee Starbuck," she said. "You sound as if you'd gone daft. If there's trouble, we'll stay right here and defend what's ours. We can shoot as well as any three men on the Bear."

He had known this was exactly what she'd say. He said, "I'll argue with you some more in the morning. Right now I've got something to tell you. Melissa and I are getting married."

Ma's big chin sagged momentarily in astonishment. She recovered immediately and said, as if she had known it all the time, "I'm glad. She'll make you a good wife, though I don't know how I'll run this place without her." She crossed the room and shook hands with Lee in her manlike way. "Make her happy. That's all I ask."

"I'll do my damnedest," he said, and thought he would have been surprised if she had kissed him, as most mothers would have done. "Melissa said you wanted to see me."

Ma dropped into a chair and folded her big hands and stared at them, very grave. She was not a woman to break down or to show emotion in any way, but he saw that she was more upset than she wanted him to know.

"There's nothing you can do, Lee," she said, "though I know you'll try. You see, Caroline left this morning to take a ride. I told her she'd better not go, but she'd been staying real close to home and I guess she had cabin fever. I thought

25

she'd be gone just an hour or so, but she ain't back yet. I'm feared Nevero's got her. That red devil's been sweet on her ever since he first seen her."

"I'll saddle up and look for her." Lee stood up and turned toward the door, then swung back. "Where'd Melissa go?"

"She's cleaning out the barn," Ma said. "I'd just started it, so she's finishing the job."

"I want to see her before I go," Lee said. "You think about going to Steamboat Springs, because I'm taking Melissa whether you go or not."

Ma's chin jutted forward in the belligerent way it always did when she was crossed. "No, you won't," she snapped. "I'm still running this family, and you'd better not forget it."

"You're not running Melissa when she's my wife," Lee said. "Don't you forget that."

"Lee." She moistened her lips and went on, "Lee, you sure it ain't Caroline you want to marry? She needs a strong man like you for a husband, and you could—"

"I'm sure," he said, and left the cabin.

When he reached the barn and saw Melissa lifting fork-fuls of manure into a wheelbarrow, he felt sick. "My God, 'Lissa," he exclaimed, "this ain't work for you to do!"

She put the fork down and shook her head. "No, it isn't," she said, "but until I'm Mrs. Lee Starbuck I'll be doing it."

"That won't be long," he said as he took the fork from her. "I wanted to tell you good-bye before I left. I'll see you tomorrow. I've got to talk to Ma some more. I didn't convince her she's got to get out of here."

When he had finished, he kissed her and held her in his arms for a moment and looked at her as he asked himself if this was real or a dream. She said softly, "Do what you have to do, Lee, but if they kill you I'll kill Caroline, because she's to blame."

"Don't do that," he said. "It would be too late."

As he strode back to his own place, he thought that it might end up with him killing both Simms and Boman, and he didn't much care if it did, not when he thought of Pa Frazer.

Chapter 6

IN LEE's opinion, Caroline Frazer was a complete bitch. As he rode downstream toward the Boman-Simms trading post, he wondered ruefully how she had ever fooled him. In her own family, only Melissa knew what she was. Pa Frazer had idolized her to the day of his death. Ma still did. Lee had heard her say a number of times, "Caroline was such a perfect baby. She just wasn't any trouble."

To Ma she was still perfect. She had a great talent for assuming an air of naive innocence, and if she was accused of even the slightest wrong doing, she would appear to be terribly hurt, and Ma would take her side. If she quarreled with Melissa she was always right, according to Ma, and Melissa was always wrong.

It would be hell to have her for a sister-in-law, Lee thought, but a man couldn't choose his in-laws any more than he could choose his own parents. He was sure she wouldn't stay on the Bear very long. She would either run away with Lucky Boman, or she would finally talk Ma into leaving this wilderness and moving back across the divide to civilization. Either would be a good thing, he told himself. Melissa would be happier if Caroline was gone, because she would be a source of irritation as long as she was in the neighborhood.

When Lee reached the trading post, he saw a lantern on the ground beside the corner of the building. He reined his black gelding to a stop and, stepping down, found Adam Simms pulling on a rope that lifted a quarter of venison to the top of a pole. This was a common and effective way of keeping meat if a man didn't have an ice house.

Simms stepped out of the light and held a gun on Lee until he saw who it was, then he said irritably, "Oh, it's you, Starbuck."

Simms was a barrel of a man, dirty and evil-smelling, who seemed to dislike everyone in the world, including his partner. They were a strange pair. Lucky Boman was a tall, handsome man who was always well groomed and could be courteous to anyone, even if he hated his insides. As far as Lee knew, the only common interest the two men had was their willingness to do anything that would make a profit.

"Boman around?" Lee asked.

"No. I just got back from a sashay onto the reservation and done a little swapping. I met up with Jack and he said he wanted to see Lucky. Claimed he had some good horses to trade. Wouldn't deal with me. Thinks he can get a better swap out of Lucky, I guess."

He had sliced off three thick steaks and had dropped them into a frying pan. Now he stopped and picked up the pan. Straightening, he added, "Wouldn't surprise me none if Jack stole them horses over in Utah and ran 'em across the line to swap to us. I told Lucky that, but he went down to look at 'em anyhow."

"You're lying," Lee said. "I think he's here."

Simms picked up the lantern and held it in one hand, the frying pan in the other. He faced Lee, his massive head drawn down into his thick shoulders, so that he resembled a huge turtle. He said sullenly, "Think what you damn please. I oughta know." He stalked past Lee into the building, and turned to where a kitchen stove stood against the wall.

Lee, following him, cast a quick glance around the littered room. Several shelves beside the stove held a variety of pots and pans, dishes, and sacks and cans of food. A fire was snapping in the stove. Simms dipped grease into the frying pan and a moment later dropped one of the steaks into the grease.

"You must be mighty hungry to tackle three steaks the size of them you cut," Lee said.

"Sure I'm hungry," Simms said, "but I don't see that it's any business of yours."

A door directly in front of Lee led into a lean-to room, and Lee was convinced that Caroline was in that room with Boman, but if he forced his way in, Simms might shoot or knife him in the back.

"If you want to buy something," Simms said uneasily, "buy it and get to hell out of here. I'm gonna eat this steak and go to bed. I've been riding all day and I'm tired."

"What are you going to do with the other two steaks?"

"They won't spoil," Simms snapped. "If I'm still hungry, I'll eat 'em. If I ain't, I'll have 'em for breakfast."

"I'll look around," Lee said. "Maybe I'll find something I want."

Simms's muddy little eyes were fixed on Lee, and the uneasiness showed in them, but he said nothing. As Lee moved along the narrow aisle between piles of hides and buckskin and bolts of calico and sacks of food, Simms forked the venison steak out of the pan and onto a plate, then he poured coffee and pulled up a chair and sat down.

Simms drew a hunting knife from its scabbard, the bright blade reflecting the light from the bracket wall lamp above him. He sliced off a big bite of the meat, harpooned it on the end of his knife, and put it in his mouth. As he chewed, blood squished from between his lips and ran down his chin into his beard.

Lee did not find any liquor, which didn't surprise him, because if Simms and Boman had some cheap trading whisky it would be hidden. He was surprised when he didn't find any rifles or ammunition, for that had been their chief trading stock for Ute hunting parties.

He stopped in front of the lean-to door, but he heard nothing that indicated Caroline and Boman were on the other side. Simms appeared to be eating with great gusto, but Lee did not doubt that the trader was watching him, and that the first sudden move on his part would bring the man's knife streaking at him like a dart. He had seen Simms throw the knife when he was showing off in front of a band of Indians. He was good, too good for Lee to take any chances on getting the steel between his shoulder blades.

"You seen any Utes lately?" he asked as he stood there.

"Yeah. Nevero and his bunch was here today. They traded for all the rifles and ammunition we had."

"How much ammunition?"

" 'Bout ten thousand rounds. Going on a fall hunt, he said."

"Hell," Lee said, "that's enough bullets to wipe out an army. You trying to—"

"Hold it right there," Simms said belligerently. "I ain't trying to do nothing. They go on a fall hunt every year. I can't go with 'em to see whether they're gonna shoot elk or soldiers. If they shoot soldiers, it proves the damned Army is fools for coming here. There ain't no law against us selling guns and ammunition to the Injuns."

That was true. Nathan Meeker had done his best to close the trading post, claiming that if the Utes could not get rifles and ammunition to hunt, they would be forced to stay on the reservation and live off the government supplies that Meeker was giving them. But Meeker had not found any way to close the post.

In a way Lee was glad, although he hated Boman and Simms and their way of doing business. In the past the Indians would have starved to death if they had been unable to hunt, because supplies had not been freighted onto the reservation. Some of the supplies had actually rotted in Rawlins warehouses because of government red tape, or lack of money, or dishonest officials. Lee had never been sure of the reason. He did know that Meeker had improved the situation, and ample supplies were now stored at the Agency.

"Simms, when did you see Caroline Frazer last?" Lee asked.

The trader rose and walked toward Lee, his knife in his hand. "Now why would you be asking that question?" he demanded.

"She's gone," Lee said loudly, wanting Caroline to hear if she was in the lean-to. "Her mother's worried. She thinks Nevero has the girl."

"Well, maybe he has," Simms said. "He always cottoned to white women. Now suppose you git, mister. I don't know what the hell you're here for, but it ain't to buy nothing."

Lee moved away from the door and Simms sidled in front of him and stood between him and the lean-to. Lee said, "I think Boman's in there. I aim to find out, so get away from the door."

"The hell I will," Simms said. "You've pussy-footed around here long enough. If you ain't out o' this building in ten seconds, I'll rip your guts out and stomp on 'em."

"I'm going in," Lee said, and moved forward as if to open the door.

Simms lunged forward, the knife making a wide sweep as he attempted to plunge it into Lee, but Lee expected him to do exactly that. He stepped back, the knife swung harmlessly past him, and then he hit Simms on the side of the head, a powerful blow that spun the man half around. He struck the trader again, this time on the jaw, and Simms went down, dazed, the knife falling from his hand.

Simms shook his head. He muttered, "You want it rough, do you?" He jerked a hand at the door of the lean-to room. "Your bucko's in there. Get rough with him if you want to. It's his fight."

Lee whirled to the door and jerked it open. Caroline was sitting on the bed and Boman was standing a few feet from her. Apparently he had expected Simms to stop Lee from opening the door, and now he was caught flat-footed.

"Well, Lee," Caroline said, "I suppose you came to rescue me from this place of sin and take me home to mother."

"That's right," Lee said. "Boman, saddle her horse for her."

"The hell I will!" Boman shouted, and whirling, he made a frantic grab for his gun that was on top of the cluttered bureau.

Lee hit him before his fingers closed over the walnut butt. Boman staggered back two steps, grunted, and then recovering his balance, rushed at Lee, fists swinging. For a time they stood there, both slugging as hard as they could, each man willing to take a blow to land one.

Lee was heavier and stronger, and he never doubted the outcome. Still he was surprised to find that Boman was quicker, just enough to make several of Lee's hard-swinging blows miss, and at the same time Boman threw some at Lee's face that landed on his nose and mouth. They cut and stung, but lacked the authority to do any real damage.

Caroline screamed, "Hit him, Lucky. Hit him again."

Lee backed through the door into the store. Boman apparently thought he had his man on the run and charged after him. Lee, both feet set, threw an uppercut that smashed past Boman's guard and, catching him on the chin, knocked him flat on his back. He lay motionless for a moment, then sat up and gently touched his chin.

Simms, sitting on a sack of sugar, said, "He licked you, Lucky."

"Get up," Lee said. "You're not licked yet."

Boman didn't move. He had turned his head to stare at Simms. He said, "I thought you were going to take care of him if he showed up."

"I tried," Simms said. "He licked me."

"All right, Boman," Lee said impatiently. "Get on your feet and saddle her horse."

Boman rose, moving very slowly as if he was badly hurt. In the thin lamplight Lee had not seen him pick up the knife Simms had dropped. Now Boman rushed him again, dropping all pretense of being injured. His right hand that held the knife swung out in a slashing blow that would have gutted Lee if it had landed, but Lee's sledging fists had jarred and slowed the man. Lee grabbed his wrist and twisted his arm, but he hung onto the knife.

For a time they strained that way, Boman swinging his left to Lee's face in a futile blow that did nothing to relieve the pressure Lee was putting on him. When he could not stand the pain any longer he dropped the knife and, stepping back, raised a foot to kick Lee in the belly. Lee grabbed his boot and upended him.

"I've played long enough," Lee said, and he stepped back so he could see Caroline, who stood in the lean-to doorway. He pulled his gun and motioned for Boman to get up. "You've got your choice, Boman. Make up your mind damned fast. You'll saddle her horse, or you'll get a slug in your brisket."

"God damn you, Lee Starbuck!" Caroline screamed. "Did you ever think that maybe Im happy living the way I do and that I like sinning and I don't want to go home to mamma?"

"You're going anyway," Lee said, "and for once she's going to hear the truth about you."

"I'll see you in hell before I—"

"Shut up." Boman was on his feet now. "I'll saddle your horse to satisfy this son of a bitch. Just remember there'll be another time."

Caroline swallowed, her angry gaze moving from Lee to Boman and back to Lee. "All right," she said finally. "There'll be another time."

On the way back she didn't say anything until they had almost reached the Frazer house. Then she spoke in a wheedling tone. "Lee, honey, you used to say you loved me. If you ever did, don't tell Ma. It'd just hurt her."

"It'll do that, all right," he said, "but maybe you're a little late thinking about it."

"No, I'm not," she flared. "I've thought of it plenty of times, but I can't get her to leave this damned place. That's why I'm going away with Lucky."

"I ain't surprised," he said. "You and Boman are sure a pair to draw to."

"Of course we are," she said smugly. "If I'd married you last summer like Ma wanted me to, I'd be stuck right here in this awful wilderness the rest of my life. I can't think of anything duller than breaking my back working eighteen hours a day for a man like you. Lucky's going to take me to

Denver and we'll live like human beings instead of working so hard every day that by night we can't do anything but go to sleep when we go to bed."

"Why haven't you left with him before," Lee asked, "instead of sneaking away to see him and lying to your ma about Nevero getting you? I suppose that's what you aim to tell her."

"Sure I will, and she'll believe me. I'll tell you why I haven't left. Lucky and Simms are selling their trading post to a man in Rawlins, but they haven't closed the deal. Besides, Lucky's got a pony herd he traded for today. He's going to drive them to Rawlins to sell, then he's coming after me."

They reached the Frazer house, and Ma, hearing them, ran out and held up her arms to Caroline, who tumbled out of the saddle and began to cry hysterically. "I thought I wasn't going to get away from the Indians," she sobbed, "but Lee rescued me. I'm tired and hungry. I lost my horse, but Lee found him, too."

"My poor baby," Ma Frazer crooned. "Come inside and I'll fix you something to eat. Lee, I don't know how we can thank you."

"He's hurt, Ma," Caroline said. "His face got cut up something awful when he fought off the Indians."

Ma Frazer stared at him, unable to see his face in the darkness. She said, "Come inside and we'll fix it up. You might get blood poisoning."

It was ridiculous and unbelievable, but it was the story of Ma's relationship with Caroline. Lee looked at Melissa, who was standing in the doorway, her strong body silhouetted against the light. Ma wouldn't believe anything he said, so there was no use to compete with Caroline's lies. Besides, Ma might be more willing now to go to Steamboat Springs than she would if she knew the truth.

"I'll be all right, Ma," he said curtly, and waved to Melissa as he rode upstream toward his place.

Chapter 7

MAJOR THORNBURGH'S command reached the junction of Fortification and Little Bear creeks by noon of Wednesday, September 24. There they found an ideal camping site with good grass and pure, sweet water, a hard combination to beat after the plodding hours they had spent crossing the Wyoming plateau.

They stayed over Wednesday night, and Thursday as well, Thornburgh deciding to make this place his supply depot. He ordered eight wagons and the one company of infantry that was in the expedition, Lieutenant Butler Price's Company E, Fourth Infantry out of Fort Steele, to remain here.

The entire operation puzzled Private Billy Buckles. He said to Amen Brown and Curly Joe Horn, "You'd think we was on a picnic, the way we're moving. My God, if the Utes are kicking up some dust and Meeker's in trouble, he'll be massacred while we sit on our butts enjoying the sunshine."

"We don't know the facts." Brown frowned thoughtfully, then added, "But then I ain't real sure the Major does, either."

"You'll smell powdersmoke soon enough, Billy," Curly Joe said.

"How do you know?" Billy asked. "The Major don't figure on smelling powdersmoke or he wouldn't be sitting around this way."

"Never ask a man like me how he knows something," Curly Joe said. "I just know. That's all."

Billy stared at him, then glanced at Amen Brown, who was staring at Curly Joe, too. A funny feeling got into Billy's spine, as if a thousand needles were picking at him. He brought his gaze back to Curly Joe, who was staring at the bulk of the mountains that was humped up against the sky to the east. Billy hadn't felt this way since his mother had died. He'd been only twelve then, but it was not a thing he would ever forget.

She had fought a high fever for days, and the doctor said

34

there was no hope for her. Billy was sitting beside the bed looking at her hot, flushed face and thinking how much he loved her and wondering how he'd make out with his three older sisters, who had always bossed him. It would be a lot worse with his mother gone.

She'd been threshing around from one side of the bed to the other, and then suddenly she stopped and was perfectly still. She lay on her back, her eyes wide open, and then she began to smile. She never moved again. It took a minute or two for him to realize she was dead; and when he did, he let out a yell that brought the family.

His oldest sister whispered, "She's crossed the bar now and she's seeing what the other side looks like. See how happy she is."

He thought it was a crazy thing for her to say, because how could his mother be happy when she was dead? He cried later, but not then. He kept staring at his mother's face. The smile had faded, but it had been there, and suddenly the little needles were pricking his spine. She had been smiling, she had been happy, and he didn't understand it at all.

Now, staring at Curly Joe's face shadowed by the brim of his campaign hat, Billy had the weird feeling that Curly Joe was smiling just as his mother had smiled when she'd died, and that Curly Joe was seeing the other side exactly as his mother had. It was crazy, but then he had a growing feeling that Curly Joe was crazy. Still, you couldn't get around what Amen Brown had said, that when something needed to be done, Curly Joe did it, and if it came to betting his last blue chip, he'd take Curly Joe ahead of anyone else. A man like that couldn't be crazy.

"Nathaniel Hawthorne once wrote in his journal something that is pertinent," Curly Joe said. "It goes like this: 'We sometimes congratulate ourselves at the moment of waking from a troubled dream: it may be so after death.' The problem is not how to die, because we all will do that whether we will it or not. The problem is how to live."

Billy walked away. He couldn't stand it. Curly Joe's quotation from Hawthorne's journal was exactly what he had thought about his mother. When she died, she looked as if she were waking from a troubled dream. Maybe that was all there was of life—an illusion that only seemed to be real. He suspected that was what Curly Joe would say if he were asked.

Not far ahead of him he saw Lieutenant Sam Cherry talking to Captain Joe Lawson. Lawson was arguing heatedly about something. A moment later Captain Scott Payne joined them and he joined in the argument. Billy remained where he was, listening and pretending not to, but he wasn't able to hear much.

Finally Lawson's words, "Damn it, we ought to be on the move," came to him. There was more argument, and then he heard Lawson's voice again: "I've never tangled with the Utes, but I have with plenty of other Indians. I just can't agree with Rankin that we'll march right through them to the Agency."

Presently Cherry and Payne turned toward Major Thornburgh's tent. Billy ran after Captain Lawson. Suddenly he had thought of the proper excuse for asking permission to ride upriver when they reached the Bear.

Billy called, "Captain," and Lawson turned. He was an old-time officer of sixty or more with an abundant growth of whiskers. He had kicked around all over the West and probably understood Indian fighting as well as anyone in the column. His red face was now even brighter than usual as the result of his argument with Cherry and Payne.

"Well?" he said gruffly.

"I know it ain't my business to offer advice," Billy said, "but I worked last summer on the Bear. I'd like your permission to make a suggestion."

"You've got it." Lawson grinned sourly. "It's time we found someone who knows enough about this country to make a sensible suggestion."

"Yes, sir," Billy said. "You see, sir, I worked for a man named Lee Starbuck who has a ranch on the Bear. He also freights supplies from Rawlins to the Agency. He knows Meeker and most of the Ute chiefs, and he could take you through this country after dark. I'd like your permission to ride up the river tomorrow and see him. If you could use him as a scout or a guide, I mean."

Lawson's sharp eyes narrowed as he chewed rhythmically on a cheekful of tobacco. Finally he said, "By God, Buckles, that is a sensible suggestion and no mistake. I'll let you know."

Billy returned to the fire. Curly Joe had disappeared, but Amen Brown was there, sprawled on the grass with his campaign hat over his eyes. He grunted something and went back to sleep. Billy, a little nervous now that he had time to consider his temerity in approaching Captain Lawson, sat down on the other side of the fire from Amen Brown and wondered what Melissa was doing, and if she had changed since he had seen her a little more than a year ago.

He wondered, too, if Lee had married Caroline. If he had, would he leave her to scout for Thornburgh? If he wouldn't, Private Billy Buckles might not be the most popular member of Company E with the old man.

Then, because he was uneasy about what Lee would say, and uneasy, too, about how Melissa would greet him, his mind turned back across the years to the months after his mother's death when he had been spoiled by his sisters, who must have thought that if they waited on him hand and foot, they would compensate for the loss of his mother. They didn't. No one—sisters or father or blonde Lucy Monroe who lived across the alley—could take the place of his mother.

He was the youngest child in the family; maybe that was why it was so hard to grow up and become a man. Or maybe it was because he was smaller than average and was picked on by the other boys in the neighborhood, and so had to fight to make a place for himself. Lucy had never cared whether he was big or little. She liked him, and she wasn't bashful about letting him know.

The best memories of his last years at home in the little eastern Kansas town had to do with Lucy. Maybe he should have stayed there and married her. Her father would have given him work in his store if he'd asked for a job. Now as he thought of her he began to recall things he had long forgotten: how small her hand was when he held it as they strolled through the warm twilights, the sweetness of her lips, the softness of her body when he had slipped an arm around her waist.

He remembered other things, too: the smell of leaves burning in the fall; the crazy things he and the neighborhood kids did on Halloween; the sweetness of a Christmas orange; the hot Fourth of July mornings when he stood beside Lucy on the street and watched the parade and had thrilled to the music of the band and tapped his foot with the music; the patriotic address by Judge Oscar Billington, who still limped from a bullet he'd taken in his knee at the battle of Wilson's Creek.

37

Now it was over. Sometimes when he thought about it he felt stunned by the suddenness with which it had ended. His sisters married and his father died and he was alone without much money from his father's estate and not yet of a mind to get married, though he knew Lucy would have married him any time he asked her.

He told Lucy good-bye and kissed her for the last time and, taking all the money that was left, caught the train to Denver. He had promised to write to Lucy, but that had been two years ago and he never had. He drifted north into Wyoming and on west to Rawlins, and then south to the Bear, where Lee hired him for the summer. When the summer was over, he joined the Army, partly because his money was about gone and three meals a day were guaranteed by Uncle Sam, but mostly because he had to fight to prove he was a man. He thought the uniform would prove it, but it hadn't. He still had to fight.

Sometimes he hated the uniform. The manufacturer had used inferior dye and the uniform was faded. Would it be a badge of glory if he wore it back to Kansas to see Lucy? He doubted it. Somehow there didn't seem to be much glory in a faded uniform which had been bleached white in the armpits and always carried the smell of body sweat and of horses. No glory at all, he thought bitterly. If Curly Joe was right and they had a fight down here in Ute country and he was killed, no one would remember him.

Lucy was probably married by now, and his sisters had their husbands and children to think about. There was just Melissa. That was why he had to see her tomorrow, to prove to her that even a small man can carve a place for himself in life and he can love as deeply as a big man like Lee Starbuck. But could he prove . . .

"On your feet, Buckles," Sergeant O'Brien bellowed. "By God, you'd think this man's army had sleeping sickness."

Billy jumped to his feet, pulled so violently out of his dreams that for a moment he swayed drunkenly as he stared at the big sergeant, whose figure was vaguely blurred at the edges.

"The Major wants to see you, Buckles," O'Brien said, "though what he's got to say to the likes of you beats me." He jerked a thumb downstream toward Thornburgh's Sibley tent. "Move now, and don't keep the Major waiting."

Billy found Major Thornburgh sitting on a camp chair

smoking a cigar. Lieutenant Cherry, seated on another camp chair, was leaning over a packing case that served as a desk. He was copying a letter that Thornburgh apparently had just finished dictating to him.

Thornburgh returned Billy's salute, his eyes moving down his short, wiry body, and then back up. He said, "Captain Lawson tells me that you know a rancher on the Bear who might assist Joe Rankin as guide."

"Yes, sir," Billy said. "Lee Starbuck. He's familiar with the country and he is well acquainted with Agent Meeker and with most of the Ute chiefs."

"I see," Thornburgh said, and was silent for a time as he drew on his cigar.

Thornburgh was about thirty-five, a tall, handsome man who had the respect of his column. Billy was glad that Thornburgh was in command, and not one of the green lieutenants just out of West Point. Still, Custer's experience as an Indian fighter had not saved him.

A man stepped into the tent. Turning, Billy saw that it was Charlie Lowry, a local man who had been hired on Tuesday as a courier when Thornburgh and Cherry had ridden up the Little Snake.

"I've been scouting around some, Major," Lowry said. "I reckon you didn't know it, but the Utes have been watching us."

"The hell!" Thornburgh said. "We're still seventy-five miles from the Agency, and that means we're a long ways from the reservation boundary."

"Don't make no difference," Lowry said. "They ain't likely to stay on the reservation now, seeing as they never have. You can be sure of one thing, Major. Them Injuns are damned interested in why you're here and what you're doing, and they'll sure keep an eye on you. What's more, they don't like the soldiers being here."

Thornburgh stepped outside and looked around. He could not imagine a more peaceful scene, with the slanting rays of the setting sun turning the hills gold and scarlet. He shook his head at Lowry and said, "I don't see any Indians."

Amused, Lowry said, "No, you wouldn't. Mostly you don't see an Injun unless he wants to be seen."

"You mean they wanted you to see them?" Thornburgh asked.

"That's about the size of it," Lowry said. "Chances are

39

they want you to know that they know you're coming. Wouldn't surprise me if Jack or Nevero or maybe Colorow didn't drop in on you about the time you get to the Bear."

"Mr. Cherry is finishing copying a letter that you will take to the Agency and deliver to Mr. Meeker," Thornburgh said. "Buckles, I want you to see this rancher tomorrow after we reach the Bear. Tell him we can use another scout, since Lowry will be riding to the Agency."

"Yes, sir," Billy said.

He walked slowly back to the fire, angling through the wagons that had been drawn up along the creek. He felt his heart thumping at the thought of seeing Melissa again. But what would she think of him and his faded uniform? Would it prove to her he was a man? Would it make her proud of him? Had she recovered from her crush on Lee? Would she hate him because he was one of the soldiers who had come here and stirred up the Utes and brought about bloodshed that might have been avoided if the Indians had been left alone?

Today he had only had questions; tomorrow he would have some answers, but there was one question that would not be answered, and that kept nagging him. Why had he gone off and left a girl who loved him and come out here and fallen in love with another girl who had never done anything to encourage him except permit him to kiss her once? He was a fool, he guessed, and that was a hell of a poor answer.

Chapter 8

LUCKY BOMAN had no illusions about his stay on Bear River. It was finished. He had had all that he could stand of dirty, coarse Adam Simms. When Simms had lain down in his fight with Lee Starbuck and as much as told him to go after Boman, he'd written "finish" to the partnership. Simms had promised to keep Starbuck from opening the lean-to door if he showed up, but he hadn't really tried. Now Boman promised himself he'd kill the bastard as sure as he smelled like a billy goat.

Besides, Boman couldn't endure the trading post or the country any longer. Sometimes he thought the silence and loneliness would drive him stark, raving mad. It would have if it hadn't been for Caroline Frazer's visits.

Now, to make it worse, he was scared. Simms, knowing the Utes and hearing their side of the trouble with Nathan Meeker, had talked about a blow-up all summer. He'd told Boman more than once that when trouble came, everyone on the Bear would have to get out fast. The killing of the first white man would simply whet the Indians' appetite for more blood.

Now trouble wasn't far off. Jack and Nevero had made that clear enough when they'd stopped to trade for all the rifles and ammunition that Simms and Boman had in the store. They wouldn't let the soldiers cross the reservation boundary, which they would certainly try to do. The soldiers were moving very slowly, so it would be several days before they reached the reservation, and in those days Boman had to accomplish several things.

Wanting time to think, he took his fishing pole and walked to the river. Fishing was one of the few pastimes he had been able to enjoy since he had thrown in with Simms, but today he didn't work very hard at it. Time was running out on him. He thought about the things he wanted to do. He told himself he had to have the filled money belt Simms wore around his waist, and it was nearly as essential to take Caroline with him when he left. He also wanted to sell the pony herd he and Simms had acquired from the Indians.

Stealing the money belt was the most important and would be the hardest. It gave him a double reason for killing Simms, but it was safer to murder a man in Denver than it was in a wilderness like this. Unless the timing and the opportunity were exactly right, the law would be on his tail, because he was obviously the one who had the most to gain. Well, he'd see that the timing and opportunity were exactly right.

Taking Caroline was no problem, because she wanted to go. He laughed when he compared the promises he had made with what he really planned to do. He'd told Caroline he'd marry her, but he didn't have the slightest intention of keeping his promise. She was the kind of woman who appealed to men, so when he got her to Denver, she'd make a lot of money for him. Oh, she'd raise hell at first, but in time she'd get used to it.

41

As far as he could see, Lee Starbuck was the real problem. The fellow would be after him as soon as Ma Frazer knew Caroline was gone. God, how he hated Starbuck! He'd like to kill him, but the truth was he was afraid of him, especially after the beating he'd taken.

Boman wished he could figure out a way to get Simms to kill Starbuck. Simms had been knocked around some by him, so he had reason enough to kill him. But Simms was a practical man. He was as anxious as Boman was to get out of the country with his life and money, so he'd say why ask for trouble just to get square with a man who had slugged him a time or two.

As for the pony herd, Boman thought he could take it north when he left with Caroline. A man named Davis was coming down from Rawlins in a few days to buy the trading post. The easiest way would be to sell the horses with the trading post, even though he would make less than if he delivered the ponies in Rawlins.

All of this depended on timing. If the Utes blew up too soon, Davis wouldn't come and Boman might have to ride off and leave the trading post and the ponies. There were just two things that were important: to get Simms's money belt and take Caroline. These he was determined to do.

When he left the river he hadn't caught any fish, and he was still gripped by indecision. Reaching the store, he was surprised to see that Simms had harnessed the team and hooked them up to the wagon.

"What the hell are you doing?" Boman demanded.

"Going out on the last trading trip we'll ever make." Simms nodded at the wagon, which held a small load of hay. "I've put all the whisky we have left in the wagon. It ain't a lot, but we don't want the soldiers finding it here. Besides, I don't figger on losing anything more'n we can help."

"I thought you had more brains than this," Boman said with pretended anger. "The way the Utes are feeling, you'll lose your hair and they'll take the whisky."

"I've always got along with 'em," Simms said. "If we wait till they've had a fight and killed some soldiers, I might lose my hair, so I ain't waiting."

"We've got a pony herd to drive to Rawlins," Boman said, still feigning anger. "And another thing. Davis is going to be here in a few days to buy the store. You ought to be on hand to dicker with him."

"I'll be here," Simms said. "And don't run off with the

pony herd while I'm gone now. If you do, I'll chase you to—"

"All right, all right," Boman said, as if exasperated. "I sure won't worry about what you'll do to me, because you're going to get killed and I won't be dividing nothing with a dead man."

Simms laughed. "I'll be back and you'll be dividing, all right. Well, it's time I was rolling or I won't get to Williams Fork tonight."

Boman stood in front of the store for a time watching while Simms forded the river and started the long climb to the south. He knew exactly what he would do. He should have thanked Simms, he thought, and he smiled. The man was as gullible and willful as a child. Now the timing and circumstances would be exactly right.

If Boman had suggested that Simms make this trip, he would have refused. Or even if Boman had agreed with him that it was a smart thing to do, he might have decided against going, so Boman had argued about it and made Simms think he was worried about his safety. Simms, being the hardhead that he was, would not turn back under any conditions.

Boman waited until Simms was out of sight, then he slipped a pair of moccasins into his pocket, saddled his horse, and, shoving his Winchester into the scabbard, rode south. He knew where Simms usually camped on Williams Fork, which would be as far as he'd have time to go before dark.

Boman left the road soon after he crossed the river and made a wide swing so that Simms would not see him. This made for slow traveling. When he reached the ridge above Williams Fork and could look down on the stream, he saw that Simms had arrived ahead of him and had already built a fire.

Glancing at the darkening sky, Boman realized he had to move fast or darkness would overtake him trying to make his way back up the slope through the brush and maybe he'd miss his horse and spend half the night trying to find the animal. He wanted to get back as soon as he could, for he hoped Caroline would visit him during the night.

He pulled off his boots and put on the moccasins. Taking his rifle from the scabbard, he moved down the slope as noiselessly as he could. Once Simms heard a rock bounce off a boulder halfway up the ridge and turned to see what

43

had jarred it loose. Boman dropped flat and stayed still for a full minute, until Simms decided no one was up there and swung back to his fire.

Boman took another five minutes to reach the bottom. When he was directly behind Simms, he raised his Winchester and without the slightest hesitation shot the man between the shoulder blades. Simms staggered under the impact of the slug and fell on his face, dead. After that Boman worked as fast as he could, not wanting some wandering band of Indians to ride in on him. If any were close enough to hear the shot, they might decide to investigate.

He killed the horses, emptied the whisky kegs into the river, and, taking the money belt from around Simms's waist, scalped and mutilated him with his own knife. Then, setting fire to the hay on the wagon, he started back up the ridge.

He reached the top before it was completely dark. He pulled his boots on, mounted, and angled down the long slant to the road. He traveled to the Bear as fast as he could, for now that it was over he began to sweat. Several freight wagons were on the road bound for the Agency, and it was possible that some of the teamsters had camped on Williams Fork close enough to hear the shot.

Caroline was waiting for him when he reached the post. "Where have you been?" she demanded. "I had to walk because I was afraid I'd wake Ma if I took a horse. We had a big row tonight. Lee's trying to get Ma to go to Steamboat Springs and she can't make up her mind. I didn't want her to hear me ride away, because she might stop believing everything I tell her."

"I had to take a little ride," he said carelessly. "Kind of a scouting trip to see if any Indians were around, but there weren't."

He kissed her in the wild, almost brutal way that stirred her, and then she asked, "When are you taking me out of this terrible country, Lucky? I can't stand it much longer."

"I can't, either," he said. "It'll be soon now. Just a day or two."

He took her home before dawn. She rode behind him, her arms around his waist. She said, "I love you, Lucky. I love you so much that if you left me I'd just die."

He laughed. "Honey, I wouldn't ride off and leave you any more than I'd hand my pony herd over to the Army for nothing. I've got to stay here another day or two until Adam

44

gets back. He's off on a trading trip. As soon as he shows up, we'll get out of here even if it means walking off and leaving the post as it stands."

"I've told Ma I wasn't going to Steamboat Springs, but suppose I can't talk her out of it?"

"I'll find you. You're my woman and I'm not leaving you to dry up in this God-forsaken wilderness." He paused, and then couldn't keep from bragging, "I've made some money since I came to the Bear. I'm going to Denver and buy a fancy layout, a combination saloon and gambling place. A lot of money is coming into Denver from the mines and we might as well get our share of it. I'll dress you in silks and satins and diamonds, and I promise you'll never have a dull day as long as you live."

She sighed. "It sounds too good to be true."

"It'll be true," he said. "You wait and see."

He helped her down from the horse before they were close enough to the Frazer house for Ma or Melissa to hear them. He kissed her and told her not to worry, that he'd find her wherever she was. Then he rode back.

He'd wait, he told himself, until someone found Simms's body and brought word that he'd been murdered by the Utes, then he'd take the pony herd and sell the post to Davis if he came as he had promised, and no one would question his right to keep all the money.

He had been named Daniel Webster Boman by his mother, but no one used the name. Someone had called him Lucky when he was a boy and the name had stuck. A good reason, too. He always had been lucky, and he still was. Now all he had to do was to make the right guess when to leave the country with Caroline; but with luck like his, he couldn't miss.

Chapter 9

LATE THURSDAY night Charlie Lowry left Thornburgh's camp on Fortification Creek to take the Major's letter to

45

Nathan Meeker. On the following morning, September 26, Thornburgh led his three companies of cavalry and twenty-five wagons south to Bear River. Here they made camp, most of the soldiers soon scattering along the bank to fish. Even Curly Joe and Amen Brown tried their luck, but Private Billy Buckles had no time for fishing. He had an errand to run.

When Billy saw the Frazer house ahead of him, his heart began to pound so that it was hard for him to breathe. He'd wanted to see Melissa for a long time, and he'd given up hope after Sergeant O'Brien had turned him down. But now he was here, and he'd be seeing her in a matter of minutes.

Ma Frazer was in the garden digging potatoes. As usual, or at least as he remembered her, she was dressed in man's clothes and doing man's work. Pa Frazer had been killed before Billy started working for Lee, so he had never seen Ma while her husband was alive; but from what Lee had said, Billy judged she had done the housework then and Melissa had helped Pa because she was a big, strong girl.

Caroline was neither big nor strong, so she worked inside. But from what Billy had seen, she didn't do much of that. This had always made Billy furious, because Melissa's hands were as calloused and hard as a man's.

There was no justice in it. If Ma couldn't afford to hire a man, she ought to give the place up, but she was too stubborn for that. He remembered Lee telling him that the Frazers had bounced all over the country for years and had never put their roots down. When they drifted over the mountains and saw Bear Valley, Pa said this was the country he had been looking for all his life.

He had been only forty-two when he staked out his quarter section beside Lee Starbuck's place. Not long after that a band of renegade Utes had cut him down for no reason except that they were drunk and mean. Now Ma Frazer would stay here and prove up on this piece of land and make it the family home, come hell or high water, simply because her husband had picked it.

Ma must have seen Billy coming, but she paid no attention to him until he pulled up at the edge of the potato patch and called, "Howdy, Miz Frazer."

She straightened and put a hand to her back. She stared at him for a moment, scowling, then she cried, "Why, it's Billy Buckles as sure as I'm a foot high." She strode across the soft earth of the garden to the sod where he had stopped his horse and shook hands with him. "I didn't know you'd joined the Army, Billy."

"Yes, ma'am," he said. "Right after I left here."

"Well, I don't cotton to the Army," Ma said, "especially right now when it's hell bent to stir up a mess of trouble, but you ain't to blame. You make a right fine-looking soldier, Billy."

"Thank you, ma'am," he said. "I came to see Lee. Major Thornburgh wants him to serve as scout. He's home, ain't he?"

"Yes, he's home, but I don't know what he'll say." Ma pushed her hat back on her forehead. "He's been doing his best to get me to leave here and go to Steamboat Springs where me and the girls will be safe, but Caroline don't want to go. I ain't made up my mind, neither. If there is trouble, the Indians will burn us out and I couldn't bear to lose my home."

"I did want to see Melissa," Billy said, "but at the same time I kind o' hoped you'd be gone. It ain't going to be safe here along the river if the shooting starts."

"Is the shooting going to start?" Ma demanded. "That's what I don't know. I keep hoping the Indians won't make no trouble when they see the soldiers; but Lee, he says that's what will set 'em off."

"I don't know, and I don't think even the Major knows," Billy said, "but I have a partner who seems to have second sight. He says there will be fighting and some of us will get killed."

"Oh, pshaw," Ma said, and she laughed. "I don't take no stock in anybody having second sight, but Lee's smart about things like this. He was to the Agency the first of the week, so maybe he knows what he's talking about."

She leaned on her fork handle for a time, her gaze touching the house and then the barn and other outbuildings that her husband had built carefully and well, saying they would last a lifetime. It was smarter, he had told her, to spend time building them than to be shipshod and have to rebuild in another ten years.

Watching her, Billy thought she was going to cry. He sensed she was remembering her husband and the shots she had heard, and how she had run out of the house to find him dead on the river bank, the dust on the other side the only trace of the Indians. He thought he understood how she felt. Her husband was buried here; his blood and sweat was part of the land, and she could not bear to leave it.

Lee, Billy knew, felt much the same about his ranch. No one had died to hold it, still it was a part of a dream and therefore a part of his life, even a part of him. Billy had never felt this great hunger to own land. Maybe he hadn't matured enough and Lee had; but now, watching Ma, he understood and began to feel a vague stirring he had never felt before. He could have found a good quarter section along the river a year ago. He would have been smarter to have settled here than to have joined the Army, but that was something he had not known at the time.

Ma seemed to wake up suddenly. She motioned toward the woodshed back of the house. "Melissa's cutting wood," she said. "I've got to get back to work."

"You're going to take the girls to Steamboat Springs, ain't you?" Billy asked. "Maybe you'll lose your buildings, but you'd still be alive."

"I'm thinking on it," she said, and then added irritably, "You sound just like Lee."

She plodded back to the row of potatoes she had been digging. He rode on to the woodshed, hearing the rhythmic strokes of Melissa's axe from the other side of the building. He dismounted and walked around the shed. Her back was to him. For a moment he watched her swing the axe with precision and strength, and a great warmth of feeling for her swept over him. He loved her. He should have told her before he left a year ago. Somehow, some way, he had to get her out of here where she was a work horse.

"Melissa," he called, and walked toward her.

She spun around, the axe still in her hands, and stared at him for a moment, then she cried, "Billy! Billy Buckles! We didn't know you were in the Army. What a nice surprise."

He reached her and put his arms around her slim body, and brought her mouth down to his. She kissed him as if she was glad to see him, and then drew back. Again he felt a blow to his pride. She had to bend to kiss him.

Still he held her, unwilling to let her go. He wanted to kiss her again, wanted to tell her he loved her and to ask her to marry him, but she pulled his arms away from her waist, smiling a little as she said, "I don't think Lee would mind if I kissed you once, but he wouldn't like it if we kept on kissing."

"Lee?" He stared at her stupidly, knowing what she meant but not believing it. He felt a great weight pressing against his chest that forced the air out of his lungs. He wanted to shout at her, but his voice came out a whisper. "What's Lee got to do with us kissing?"

"A lot of things can change in a year, Billy," she said gently. "Lee and I are getting married in a few days, probably as soon as we get to Steamboat Springs."

"But it was Caroline . . ."

"I told you a lot of things change in a year," she said, still smiling. "It used to be Caroline, but it isn't now."

He looked at her, blinking back tears that threatened to roll down his cheeks. He turned away, not wanting her to see, not wanting her to even know how he felt. It wasn't right. All this time he had loved her, but he had come too late and she was spoken for. Lee should have been satisfied with Caroline; but no, he had to take Melissa, who . . .

He heard her voice, sounding low and far away, "You look fine, Billy. Are you stationed at Fort Steele?"

"Yes," he said, his own voice sounding strange to him. "Company E, Third Cavalry. We're camped down the river not far from the trading post. Is Lee home? I've got to see him."

"I haven't seen him today," she said, "but I'm sure he is. What do you have to see him about?"

"Army business."

She smiled, ignoring his curt tone. "I'm glad I had a chance to see you, Billy."

"I'm glad I saw you," he said, and hurried past the woodshed to where he had left his horse.

He mounted and rode around the front of the house so that he would not see her. Then the tears came. For an instant he was a little boy again, hating Lee Starbuck, who had everything, even the girl Billy loved.

Well, this made Private Billy Buckles the biggest fool who ever put on one of Uncle Sam's uniforms. Only a fool would take a girl like Melissa for granted; only a fool would think that putting on a uniform would make him six feet tall in Melissa's eyes. He was a runt, and that's what he would be all his life.

He wiped a sleeve across his eyes and straightened in the saddle. He set his jaw, glad he had not told Melissa how he felt, glad that Lee didn't know. Anyhow, it would be hell married to a girl as tall as Melissa.

Chapter 10

LEE HAD just snaked a cottonwood drift log from the north bank of the river to the rear of his cabin when he saw a soldier leave the Frazer house and ride toward his place. He started to drive his team back to the river where there was another log he wanted to saw up for winter wood; then he stopped, thinking there was something familiar about the small trooper who was riding toward him.

One thing was sure. The cavalry had arrived in Bear Valley or this soldier wouldn't be here. Trouble had finally come, the kind of trouble that Jack had hoped Lee could prevent. Then he wondered what business the Army had with him. The thought that the Army had *any* business with him made him uneasy.

He didn't recognize the soldier until he reined up and stepped down, then the narrow face and the sharp little nose and chin and the quick, catlike way he moved told Lee who he was. He shouted, "Billy! Billy, how in hell did you ever manage to get into that monkey suit?"

Lee held out his hand and Billy took it, trying to smile, but his face was frozen and the smile didn't quite come. He said, "I enlisted right after I left here, Lee. I couldn't find a job in Rawlins and I was about out of money, so I joined up. I figured that was one way to eat regular."

Lee pumped Billy's hand and slapped him on the back. "You knew you could have stayed the winter with me if it was just a case of eating regular."

"Well, a man gets a little money riding for Uncle Sam," Billy said. "It ain't so bad in some ways, though I may think different before we get to the Agency."

"That where you're headed?" Lee asked. "Billy, that's one sure way to die young. How big an outfit is it?"

"Three companies of cavalry," Billy answered. "The Major left some of the wagons and one company of infantry on Fortification Creek for his supply depot."

"And you're going clean on to the Agency?"

"I ain't sure," Billy admitted. "This is where you come in.

I don't know what the Major's orders are. He don't go around telling us or asking advice, but I've got a hunch he needs advice from a man like you who knows what he's talking about. He wants you to serve as a guide."

"Guide?"

Lee stared at Billy. His first inclination was to laugh. He had never served as a guide or scout with the Army in his life, and in many ways he had only contempt for soldiers and officers, who were under orders and therefore were unable to use their own judgment or initiative. He shook his head, seeing Billy's grave expression and knowing it was a thing he could not laugh at.

"Not me," Lee said. "I'm a freighter and a rancher, but I sure as hell ain't no guide for the Army."

"You know who we got now?" Billy demanded. "Joe Rankin, a livery-stable owner. He's dressed up in fancy buckskin and talks as if the Utes are a bunch of cowards who won't fire a shot. I don't believe it. You've got to take the job, Lee, or chances are we'll get ambushed between here and the Agency."

"I know Joe," Lee said thoughtfully. "He's solid enough, and he's been over the country. He'll take you soldier boys where you want to go. That's all I could do."

"No, it ain't," Billy said. "That's why I told 'em about you. It's more'n following the road and taking us to the Agency. I ain't going to criticize the Major or his officers, but the truth is none of 'em know the Utes. They've done some Injun fighting—Captain Lawson has anyhow, but it's been mostly Plains tribes, and the Utes are different. You've told me that a dozen times."

"Yeah, that's true enough," Lee admitted, "but I've got this place to look out for. I've been trying to talk the Frazer women into going to Steamboat Springs." He shook his head. "No, I'll have to turn it down."

"I'll be in a hell of a lot of hot water if you turn it down," Billy said. "I volunteered for you, I guess you'd say. I've listened to Rankin talk and I tell you we need you. The Major thinks so, too, or he wouldn't have sent me."

Lee shook his head again. "I'm mindful of all that, Billy, but my God, this is a terrible mistake. Meeker made it. The Indian Department made it. Now the Army's making the last one. All it'll take for the Utes to blow up is for the soldiers to move in. I seen Jack and Nevero on my way back from the Agency. Jack made it plenty plain."

Billy put out a hand to grip Lee's arm. He said hoarsely, "All right, it don't make you no never mind whether my friends and Major Thornburgh and me die. We take that risk when we join and I ain't belly-aching about it, but there's something else you'd better think about. Maybe you can convince the Major the Utes will fight and he'd better stay here, or at least not go south of Williams Fork. You might be able to stop a fight. If you don't, you can lose your place. So can the Frazers and everybody else along the Bear."

Lee drew a cigar from his pocket and bit off the end. He put it into his mouth and chewed on it for a time, then he asked, "You really think the boys with the brass buttons would listen to me?"

"Sure they will," Billy said, "or they wouldn't have sent me up here to see you."

Lee tongued the cigar to the other side of his mouth and took another grip on it. If there was the slighest chance of stopping the war with the Indians he'd be a fool not to take it, especially after what Jack had told him on his way home. Still, he could not believe that the officers would listen to him, especially if their orders were to cross the reservation boundary and go on through Coal Creek Canyon to the Agency. They'd never get out of that canyon alive. If he went with them, he'd die along with the men in uniform.

But there was a chance, and so it seemed to him he had no choice. "All right, Billy," he said. "I'll go, but it'll take a little time. I want to stop at the Frazers, too. If Ma still is determined not to leave, I can't go. I've got to stay here and do the best I can to look out for 'em."

"I savvy that," Billy said. "I'll help you unharness."

It was not until after the team had been turned into the pasture and Lee's black had been saddled that Billy burst out: "I seen Melissa when I rode past the Frazer house. She says you and her are getting married."

Lee nodded as he tied his blanket roll behind the saddle. "As soon as we can. That's one reason I didn't want this damned job you so kindly volunteered for me. I figured to take her to Steamboat Springs and we'd get married there."

He turned to see Billy staring at him, his eyes narrowed. He stood motionless, shocked by the hatred he saw in Billy's face, the kind of hatred that lies deep inside a man and festers there until it poisons him.

"What is it, boy?" Lee asked. "What's eating on you?"

"I was thinking how it was a year ago," Billy said. "You was in love with Caroline then. I thought you was going to marry her. You said Melissa was just a girl. I don't see how you could quit loving Caroline and start loving Melissa. I mean, I never thought love was something you turned off and on like that."

"It ain't," Lee said. "I guess I never really loved Caroline. She's got a pretty face and a way of switching her hips that makes a man's mouth water, but when I started thinking ahead—well, she wasn't for me."

"But if you loved her——" Billy began wildly.

"That's what I'm saying," Lee broke in. "I didn't. Love ain't all purty sunsets and romances and sitting around crocheting lace for a tablecloth. When you fall in love and figure to get married, your woman's got to be willing to work as hard as you do. It's having your babies, and maybe dreaming the same dreams. . . ."

A new and startling thought hit him so hard that he stopped, wondering if he had suddenly gone out of his mind. He sensed the truth, yet he couldn't believe it. Billy Buckles was in love with Melissa, and now he was so jealous he was half crazy with it. Then another idea bit into Lee's mind. Maybe Billy wanted him to join Thornburgh's column so he could shoot him in the back if a fight started, and get him out of his way.

No, that was crazy. Billy Buckles, who had worked for him last summer, wouldn't, or couldn't, do it. But that had been a year ago. The Army did things to men. Lee had seen it happen time after time. This was Private Billy Buckles of the United States cavalry, who had probably spent a year thinking about Melissa and believing he was in love with her. Now, suddenly, he learned she was to marry another man. It wasn't crazy, not as crazy as Lee wanted to think.

"We'd best be riding," he said, and stepped into the saddle.

They rode downstream in silence, Lee wondering if he would ever see his place again. Or would he be alive to see it? He glanced at Billy's stormy face and then stared ahead again. There was a good chance he wouldn't come back, he thought; a very good chance with the Utes in front of him and Billy Buckles behind him.

Chapter 11

WHEN Lee and Billy reached the Frazer house, Billy refused to go in. "I'll wait here," he said stubbornly as he stared downriver. Rather than argue, Lee dismounted, and stepping up on the porch he knocked at the door.

Melissa opened the door. She said, "Come in," and smiled at Lee the way a woman does who knows she is loved by the man she loves. Glancing past Lee, she asked, "Doesn't Billy want to come in?"

"He said no." Lee saw that Caroline was sitting next to a window sewing, and Ma Frazer was in the kitchen having a cup of coffee. In a low tone he said, " 'Lissa, did you know that Billy's in love with you?"

"Did he tell you so?" she asked.

"No, but I figured it out. He said you'd told him we were getting married, and he was mad. He said I was in love with Caroline last year and he didn't see how I could turn it off and on this way."

Melissa laughed softly. She said, her voice barely loud enough to reach Caroline, "If he knew my sister, he'd know how you could turn love off."

Caroline's head snapped up, a petulant expression on her face. She got up, her sewing in her hands, and without a word of greeting to Lee, stalked into her room and slammed the door.

His gaze followed her until the door closed, then he said, "I still don't savvy her, 'Lissa. She's smart, and she's pretty enough to make a man look at her whether he wants to or not. She could have a decent life, so why is she bound to throw it away on a man like Boman?"

"She could have had a decent life with you, couldn't she?" Melissa asked.

He thought he caught a hint of envy in her voice. He shook his head. "No. I knew I didn't love her even before I found out how she felt about Boman. It's like I told Billy. When you fall in love, you want your girl to like the things

54

you do and live where you do and be willing to work as hard as you do." He hesitated, and then added, "I said that having a man's babies and dreaming the same dreams . . . "

"Oh, honey." She drew him away from the door so Billy couldn't see them and kissed him. "I want to do all of those things. You know I do. Most of all I want to have your babies."

"It's just that I love you, not Caroline," he said. "It never was her, really. At least not after I saw that you had become a woman. . . . Come on. I've got to talk to Ma."

He took Melissa's hand and they went into the kitchen. Ma looked at Lee, her expression a little sour, he thought. She said, "I'm tired. I've been digging potatoes all day and I've got some more to dig. I guess I'm getting old, Lee. Why don't you love birds quit kissing and get married and start doing the work around here?"

"Don't answer till I fetch you a cup of coffee, Lee," Melissa said. "It's black enough to give you strength, and you need it when Ma talks that way."

"It's black, all right," Ma said. "She don't have to fetch it to you. It'll come if you call it."

He laughed as he dropped into a chair at the table. "I can use the coffee, all right, but I'm ready to answer Ma even before I get it. I'm ready to quit kissing and get married. So's Melissa, but there's a little problem we'd best get settled. The Army's here. We know that means trouble. Billy came to get me to scout for 'em."

"I know," Ma said. "He told me."

"You can't, Lee," Melissa said. "You just can't." She stopped halfway between the stove and the table, the cup of coffee in her hand. "We were going to Steamboat Springs to be married. This is the Army's business, not yours. You might get killed."

"That's right," Lee said. "But I might get killed right here, too. Now if you'll bring that coffee . . ."

"I'll pour it down your neck if you do it," she said as she set the cup in front of him. "Of all the stupid ideas . . ."

"Maybe not," Lee said. "Billy put it to me kind of tough. He says I might be able to talk Thornburgh into staying on the Bear, or at least not going past Williams Fork. If I can do that, I might be able to stop the war. If I can't, we'll have it sure."

"Does the Army ever listen?" Melissa demanded. "Do you think Custer listened to anybody?"

Lee shrugged. "Maybe Thornburgh's different from Custer. Anyway, it looks to me as if I've got to try. If I didn't, and it turns out bad, I'd always be to blame. Or at least I'd blame myself. Besides, I can talk to Jack maybe better than anyone, and he'll make the decision. There's just one thing, Ma. Are you taking the girls to Steamboat Springs?"

"It's Caroline," Melissa broke in angrily. "She won't budge. She won't give any reason. She just can't go yet, she says."

"All right, all right." Ma held up a hand. "I ain't slept much since that day the Injuns had her. I sure can't figure her out. After an experience like that, you'd think she'd be so scared she'd want to go, but she's bound to stay here for another two or three days."

"I can tell you why," Lee said, "but you wouldn't believe me."

"I wouldn't believe you if what you said didn't jibe with what she said," Ma agreed. "I won't believe she lies to me. I can't, Lee. Whatever she'd do, she wouldn't lie."

Lee glanced at Melissa and saw that she was close to crying. Quickly he brought his gaze back to Ma. This was the first time he had ever heard her admit that Caroline was anything less than perfect. The admission had been hard for her to make. He saw no reason to push her. She was unhappy enough as it was, probably because she sensed the truth but still refused to accept it.

"Are you going to make her go with you?" Lee asked. "I have to know. If you ain't, I'll take Melissa to Steamboat Springs and we'll get married. If you're going, you and the girls will be safe and I'll go talk to Thornburgh."

Ma put her big, calloused hands on the table and clenched them into fists so tightly that the knuckles were white. He suspected that she had never *made* Caroline do anything in her life, and she was reluctant to try to now. Perhaps she wasn't sure she could do it.

"We'll go," she said. "But I'd rather stay here and die trying to keep the home Pa built for us. It was the first real home we ever had and we would have lived here the rest of our lives and been happy. Lee, I just can't bear it if we're burned out while we're gone. It's all we've got of Pa." She swallowed, and moistened dry lips, then she said, "But after what happened to Caroline, I can't take the risk of staying."

Lee finished his cup of coffee and stood up. "All right, Ma. Just don't stay here too long."

Melissa walked with him to the front door. Lee said in a low voice, "She knows about Caroline and Boman, don't she?"

"I think so," Melissa said. "She's no fool, though she acts like one as far as Caroline is concerned, but I guess she'd go crazy if she admitted it to herself, hating Boman like she does. She's always blamed him for Pa's murder, so if Caroline runs off with him . . ."

She stopped, unable to go on, but he understood. He said, "If I know her at all, she'll get to him unless you lock her up. Don't let Ma put off going. It's my guess you've got maybe one day of grace—not more'n two at the most. If Thornburgh goes to Williams Fork tomorrow and camps there, you may have till Sunday morning. Don't let her put it off any longer."

"I'll try," Melissa said, "but you know Ma. She's real practical about everything except Caroline."

"I don't figure to be gone more'n four, five days," he said. "I'll find you in Steamboat Springs."

He drew her to him and kissed her, and she became a living flame in his arms. She could not get enough of his lips. She pressed against his strong body, her arms around him as she was held in his embrace, and when she finally drew her lips away from his, she whispered, "Honey, come back. Please come back."

"I will," he said, and wheeled away from her and left the house.

He mounted and rode downstream, Billy beside him. Billy glanced at him, then turned his head away, saying nothing. Lee didn't talk, either. He had no thought for Billy, or for Caroline, or even for Ma. Just for Melissa, and the terrifying possibility that he might not be able to keep the promise he had made to her.

Chapter 12

LEE AND BILLY reached camp late in the afternoon. Billy took him to the Sibley tent and introduced him to Thornburgh and then left. Thornburgh, in turn, introduced Lee to Captains Payne and Lawson, and then to Lieutenant Cherry.

He motioned for Lee to sit on one of the camp chairs and offered him a cigar, his gaze sweeping Lee's long-boned body. He nodded, as if pleased by what he saw.

"Buckles tells me you know the Ute chiefs personally," Thornburgh said.

Lee nodded. "I know the ones who'll give you trouble."

He instinctively liked Thornburgh, and he sensed that the officer was a man who could be talked to. Lawson was a thorny old-timer who might prove a little too quick on the trigger. Payne did not look well; he was pale and overweight, and Lee wondered why he had been brought on an expedition like this one, which might be a very tough one before the column returned to Fort Steele. Cherry was younger and remained in the background, so Lee was instinctively drawn to him.

Thornburgh rolled his cigar between his fingers, his gaze on Lee. He said, "Which ones will give us trouble, Starbuck?"

"Jack and Nevero," Lee said, "and maybe Colorow, although he's probably more bluff than real threat."

"I see," Thornburgh said. "Two of them were here this afternoon. Rankin told me they were Jack and Sowerwick."

"Nevero wasn't with them?"

Lee was uneasy as he thought about it. Apparently Nevero and Jack had separated, which very likely meant that Nevero had joined his band. What he would do now was a question, but there was a good chance that when the soldiers moved south Nevero would attack the ranches. The Frazer women might not have as much time as he had told Melissa they'd have. He wished he'd insisted on them leaving in the morning.

Thornburgh continued to watch him closely. Now he asked, "What are you thinking?"

"I'm worrying about Nevero," Lee said. "He's mean. Jack ain't. He's the important chief, and he's the one who will lead the fighting if there is any; but Nevero's the kind who'll sneak around your command and attack the settlers." He hesitated, and then he asked, "Could you leave one company here to patrol the river and protect the settlers?"

Thornburgh shook his head. "Custer divided his command. I have no desire to let this expedition turn out like the one on the Little Big Horn. What about this Sowerwick?"

"He'll go along with Jack," Lee said. "I returned from the Agency the first of the week. While I was camped on my way home Jack and Nevero showed up. Jack had a message for me to take to you, but I didn't take it because I figured you had your orders and what Jack said wouldn't change what you could do."

"That's right," Thornburgh said, "but what was the message?"

"He knew that Meeker had sent for soldiers and he wanted you to know that the Utes would fight. It seems that they're afraid you'll put them in chains and send them to Florida. Meeker may have threatened them with just such a punishment. I guess all of them, even old Douglas, would rather fight and die right here than go to Florida."

"I would, too, if I was a Ute," Lawson said. "Starbuck, if we were fighting the Sioux or Cheyennes or almost any other tribe, we'd have some idea what to do, but the Utes are an unknown quantity. Rankin says we've got to watch out for tricks, but they won't really fight."

"Joe's wrong," Lee said. "They'll fight if you push south. This is the main reason I'm here. I didn't want the job, because I've got work to do and three women who live on a ranch next to mine will need me if there's trouble, and there will be if you keep moving toward the reservation."

"You seem sure of that," Payne said, and he sounded irritated.

"I am sure," Lee said. "If there is trouble, some of the bands, probably Nevero's, will kill all the settlers they can. I don't want the buildings on my ranch burned. I don't want my neighbors killed." After a moment's hesitation he added, "One of the women who lives next to me is my future wife."

"You want us to stay here?" Thornburgh asked.

"That's right," Lee said. "At least don't go farther south than Williams Fork."

"You'd better know right now that we can't do that," Thornburgh said. "I've already sent a letter by courier to Meeker saying we'll be at the Agency on the twenty-ninth."

Lee spread his hands as if he saw no hope. He said, "You'll never get through Coal Creek Canyon, and Meeker and his people will die. I can promise that; but if you stop on this side of the reservation boundary, I don't think anything will happen more than has already happened."

"You don't think," Payne said sharply. "I notice you don't promise that."

"If I'd had a chance to talk to Jack this afternoon, I could have made such a promise," Lee said.

"Why are you so sure there will be trouble if we keep going?" Thornburgh asked.

"What did Jack say this afternoon?" Lee responded.

"Well," Thornburgh answered, "he said that Meeker had tried to make them farm and to put their children in school. He claimed Meeker blamed them for the forest fires they've had in Colorado and told them they couldn't go on their fall hunt because they had started those fires. Jack said the fires were started by lightning and by white men."

Thornburgh stopped, but Lieutenant Cherry added, "He claimed Meeker said one thing one time and another the next time."

Lee nodded. "I think that is true. In fact, everything Jack told you was true."

Thornburgh shrugged. "I couldn't discuss Meeker with him. Right or wrong, that isn't the Army's business."

"But it is the Army's business to save Meeker's life," Lee said; "and you won't do that if you lead your column down Coal Creek Canyon to the Agency. . . . You want to know why I'm sure the Indians will fight. All right, I'll tell you. First, I know Jack. He was raised by a Mormon family and he scouted for General Crook. He's been to Denver. He knows what happened at Sand Creek and what Custer did on the Washita, so he's got reason to distrust the whites. Second, trouble's been building up here for years. Now it's ready to explode. All it'll take is for you to move your command across the reservation boundary."

He saw that they were impressed, but the situation was out of the officers' hand as much as it was out of his.

Thornburgh said, "I'm sorry, Starbuck, but we can't protect Meeker by staying fifty miles from the Agency." He offered his hand. "May I say I'm glad you're with us, and that you'll find me willing to listen any time you have a suggestion."

Lee shook hands and left the tent. He mounted and went looking for Billy's fire, thinking bitterly that he might as well have gone to Steamboat Springs with Melissa. A series of mistakes had been made, and now neither he nor the officers nor Nathan Meeker himself could undo them.

He found Billy's camp and was introduced to Curly Joe Horn and Amen Brown. Brown was a typical cavalryman, lanky and leather-faced, but Horn was something special. Lee had never met anyone like him. His gentle eyes were the saddest Lee had ever seen, and when Lee shook hands with Curly he had the startling feeling that the man was looking at him and through him and beyond him.

"I've heard Billy speak of you," Curly Joe said pleasantly. "I'm glad you've joined us. Now we will all meet our destiny together. We can neither stop it nor dodge it."

Lee ate supper with them, sharing their coffee and bacon and hard bread. Later, after Curly Joe left them to try his luck on the river bank, Amen Brown said to Lee, "He's a strange one, now ain't he?"

Lee nodded. "What's the matter with him?"

"Well," Brown said thoughtfully, "there ain't nothing really the matter with him. It's us. We don't savvy him. I've read the Bible and even done a little preaching in my time, but he knows the Book a lot better'n I do."

Brown scratched his stubble-covered cheek, and went on, "He's fought Injuns and lost his scalp a long time ago. He don't never talk about it, but that must o' been what happened. Sometimes, hearing him talk, I get the feeling we're all marching to hell together on this trip."

"We may be," Lee said.

Presently Brown drifted away and Lee squatted beside Billy. He filled his pipe and lighted it with a burning twig, then he said, "I came along like you asked me to. I ain't sure I done right, but I came, though it don't look like I can say anything to keep Thornburgh from going on through to the Agency. Now I want to know something. Why are you acting like a God-damned spoiled sullen brat?"

Billy looked at him, his face turning red. He raised a fist as if he wanted to hit Lee, but he dropped it. He muttered, "You wouldn't savvy."

"I figure I would," Lee said. "I'm guessing, but I think it's because you're in love with Melissa yourself. I don't blame you, boy. I'm lucky to have her love me."

Billy bowed his head, his thin shoulders shaking. Several minutes passed before he was able to speak. "You guessed it, all right. I fell in love with her last summer, but I didn't do nothing or say nothing to her. I didn't have anything to get married on. Then when we got here, I hit on the idea of fetching you to guide the column, but what I really wanted was a chance to see Melissa. I did, and when she told me you and her was getting married, I felt like the sky had dropped on top of me."

"And maybe the notion occurred to you that if we had a fight and you shot me, you'd have a chance with 'Lissa?"

"It occurred to me, all right," Billy said.

"Some of us are going to get killed," Lee said. "It don't

take no Curly Joe Horn to tell us that. If I'm one that gets it, I want you to see what you can do for 'Lissa. She's going to need some looking out for."

Billy raised his head and looked at Lee. "You mean that?"

"I mean it," Lee said.

"I will," Billy said. "I sure will."

Lee had tried to remove one worry, but he wasn't sure he had. In any case, it had been a small one. The big worry remained. Nevero and his band would come after Caroline, and they would take Melissa too, or kill her, if Ma broke her promise and stayed on the ranch instead of going to Steamboat Springs. She would keep her word, he told himself; and yet, knowing Caroline and how Ma felt about her, he wasn't sure.

Chapter 13

LEE RODE OUT of camp early Saturday morning and forded the Bear and rode south before the column was under way. Thornburgh kept Rankin with him and ordered Lee to scout the country beyond Williams Fork. If Lee got the slightest hint that the Utes were gathering in force anywhere between the reservation boundary and Williams Fork, he was to return at once and report to Thornburgh. Lee sensed that the Major was still thinking of what had happened on the Little Big Horn, and was determined to avoid a similar catastrophe.

He returned to Williams Fork late in the afternoon to find that Rankin had discovered Adam Simms's body lying beside the charred remains of the wagon and the dead horses. Rankin had returned to the column and reported to Thornburgh. When Lee arrived, the Major along with Captain Payne and Lieutenant Cherry were studying the ground around the body.

"The first blood has been shed, Starbuck," Thornburgh said. "Did you find anything?"

Lee shook his head. "It's like always. You get a feeling that they're watching us, but you don't see them. It's my guess that Jack left a few scouts up yonder on the ridges to keep an eye on us and he went back to the Agency."

"Why?" Thornburgh asked.

"Maybe to tell Douglas and the rest of the Utes that you're moving south," Lee said. "Or maybe just to find out what's been happening to Meeker." He nodded at Rankin and motioned to the body. "How do you read this, Joe?"

"Simple enough," Rankin said. "Simms was on his way to the reservation to trade and some glory-hunting Ute buck rubbed him out."

There was no use for Lee to go over the ground after Rankin and the three officers had ridden their horses across it and had dismounted and walked around the body; but as he stared at the trader's blood-caked face, he sensed that something was out of tune. He felt that Rankin had made an error in judgment. He could not put his finger on it for a moment, then he remembered hearing that Simms always carried a heavy money belt around his waist.

"Was there anything of value on him?" Lee asked. "A filled money belt maybe?"

Rankin shook his head, frowning. "But there should have been," he said. "I just now thought of something, Lee. Simms used to come to Rawlins to buy supplies or to fetch some buckskin or maybe a pony herd to sell, and there was considerable talk that he was a walking bank. A couple of times some toughs tried to rob him, but it didn't pay. After that they left him alone."

Lee turned to Thornburgh. "I don't think the Indians did this," he said.

"Oh, come on now," Cherry said. "No white man would treat a body like that."

"You don't know what some of the whites around here would do," Lee said, "particularly if they wanted it to look like the Utes had done it."

"It was a one-man job," Rankin said. "Lee might be right, Major. It ain't likely an Injun would take his money, but I couldn't find no tracks except some moccasin prints. Looks like Simms was shot in the back from the brush. If it was a white man, he had pulled off his boots and put on moccasins."

"Sounds wild to me," Thornburgh said, as if dismissing the whole matter. "Lieutenant, we'll camp upstream from here. See that a burial detail takes care of the body."

"Yes, sir," Lieutenant Cherry said.

Lee stared at the brushy slope to the north. He said to Rankin, "Joe, there's just one good guess about who shot him. Do you make the same guess I do?"

"If a white man done it," Rankin said, "I'd figure it'd be Lucky Boman. He'd know that the money belt had enough in it to make the chance of getting his neck stretched worth the risk, and he'd probably know where Simms figgered to camp."

"It makes sense," Lee said. "Let's take a sashay yonder to the top of the ridge. If Boman did it, the chances are he left his horse up there while he worked his way down the slope to get close to Simms before he shot him."

"You go take the look," Rankin said. "I'd best stay here with the Major in case some of them red bastards show up." He cocked his head at the sun, which was far over to the west. "Better get a move on if you're gonna find any tracks afore dark."

Lee mounted and angled back and forth up the slope to the ridge top, picking his way through the brush and boulders. When he reached the crest, he tied his horse and began to search. It was not long before he found the spot where the killer apparently had left his horse. He studied the ground for a long time, starting with a wide circle and steadily closing in.

He was sure of two things. The horse was shod, and the rider had worn boots. Rankin had made a good guess. The killer had slipped on moccasins to throw suspicion on the Indians. He had been reasonably certain that his tracks could not be followed on the hard ground of the hillside, and it had probably never occurred to him that anyone would start looking on top of the ridge.

Lee judged that the killer had come in from the north, and after murdering Simms had mounted and ridden west for a time. Leading his horse, Lee followed the tracks as long as there was enough light, then he mounted and in the deepening twilight rode down the slope to the river.

The killer had angled toward the road, Lee thought, probably to save time. If it had been Boman, he would want to get back to the trading post as soon as possible, perhaps to establish an alibi. Caroline, Lee thought, would give Boman one if she had been waiting for him there.

Darkness had fallen by the time Lee reached Thornburgh's tent. Captains Payne and Lawson were standing at the edge of the stream talking to Joe Rankin in low tones. Lee stepped into the tent to find the Major sitting in a camp chair smoking a cigar, trouble a heavy burden upon him. Lieutenant Cherry was leaning over a packing case writing a dispatch.

When Thornburgh saw Lee, he snatched the cigar from his mouth and demanded, "Where have you been?"

"Tracking Adam Simms's killer," Lee said. "I found the spot where he left his horse. It was a white man, all right. He wore boots and his horse was shod. I trailed him from there until the light was too thin. He angled toward the road, and I figured he must have headed for it so he could get back to the Bear as fast as he could."

"What's this got to do with us and the Indians and Meeker?" Thornburgh asked. "You're supposed to scout for us, not run down a murderer."

"I have been scouting for you," Lee said patiently. "If you and your officers fell into this trap, and that's what it amounts to, and you figured this was an Indian killing, it wouldn't take much to make you start shooting."

Thornburgh turned the thought over in his mind, then nodded slowly. "All right, it was a white man; but either way, we're not going to be trigger happy."

"I think it's a pretty safe guess that Boman killed his partner for his money," Lee said. "I suggest you send a detail back to the Bear and arrest him. He'll probably be at the trading post."

Thornburgh shook his head. "Arresting civilian law-breakers is not our job." He lifted a sheet of paper that was on his lap and slapped it against his left hand. "While you were gone, a man named Eskridge arrived from the Agency with a letter from Meeker. It's dated September 27. That's today. He says the Utes are worked up about our coming and consider it an act of war." He paused. "I guess that's about what you told me last night."

"I knew how they felt," Lee said.

"Well, Meeker says the main thing now is to allay apprehension. The Utes want us to camp, and he says for me and five men to come on to the Agency and have a talk. We had a conference while you were gone. What would your advice have been if you had been here?"

Lieutenant Cherry stopped writing and straightened up, his eyes fixed on Lee's face. Thornburgh, too, was watching him closely. Lee thought about it a moment, knowing what he would have said if he had been here, but not knowing what decision had been made.

"I might add that you were right in guessing Jack had returned to the Agency to tell Douglas we were coming," Thornburgh said. "From what Eskridge says, I judge that is the reason for Meeker's anxiety."

"You can't be sure what a Ute is going to do when he gets excited," Lee said, "any more than you can be sure what the weather is going to be tomorrow, but I'd say that if you go in with five men and talk to Jack and the other chiefs there's a good chance you can stop a war. On the other hand, if you move onto the reservation with your command, you've got war sure."

"You say that if I take five men and go to the Agency," Thornburgh said, "I might prevent a war; but then again I might get killed, along with the five men I take and everyone at the Agency."

"That's the size of it," Lee said. "It's a gamble, but I think the odds are in your favor."

"A soldier can't ask for any more," Thornburgh said, smiling slightly. "If there is a war, the odds might not be that good."

"I'd say they'd be a hell of a lot worse," Lee said. "This is Ute country. They know every hill and valley and creek, and they know exactly where to ambush you, if it comes to that. They don't come rushing in like the Plains tribes do. I guess it's a matter of not admiring bravery just for bravery's sake; but don't make the mistake of thinking they're cowards. The thing is that if a fight is forced onto them, they'll likely fight from cover, and they're good shots."

Thornburgh's cigar had gone out. He struck a match and held the flame to the cigar as he puffed, his gaze still on Lee's face. He said finally, "I'm taking Meeker's suggestion, although Captain Payne argued strongly against it. What you've just said bears out my feelings in the matter." He nodded at Lieutenant Cherry. "I just finished dictating a message to Meeker that will go to him tonight. I'm informing him we'll move as far as Milk Creek, and the column will remain there while I go on to the Agency with the five men."

"I think that's the proper decision," Lee said.

But afterwards as he hunkered beside Billy Buckles and ate his supper, he wasn't sure what the proper decision was. They watched him, Billy and Amen Brown and Curly Joe Horn, their tired faces red in the firelight. They were wondering, he thought, if he knew any more about what was happening than they did.

"We was on the burial detail," Brown said. "I've been in the Army quite a spell, but I never seen what Injuns do to a man before. I tell you, Starbuck, it turned my insides to ice. I couldn't eat nothing when we got done."

"I wasn't any better," Billy said. "You read about things like that and you hear men talk about it, but seeing it is different."

Only Curly Joe seemed untouched by what they had seen. He sipped a cup of coffee as Lee said for the third time, "Damn it, the Utes didn't do it. Simms was worked on by a white man."

Neither Billy nor Amen Brown believed him. They seemed to be convinced he was lying, perhaps because the officers had told him to, not wanting the men to panic with the thought that this was what would happen to them if there was a fight and some of them were killed. Only Curly Joe believed him, and for the first time Lee gave serious thought to Billy's notion that the man possessed second sight.

Curly Joe set his cup down. He seldom smiled, and when he did now, his face was transformed by a gentleness that amazed Lee. He gazed at Lee as if convinced that here was a man who understood him.

"There is an Irish proverb that says, 'He that's born to hang need not fear the water,'" Curly Joe said. "Only a foolish man tries to run from his own destiny. I knew a soldier who was scared of lightning. He left his home in Illinois where they had bad thunderstorms and came out here to get away from it. He didn't. Lightning struck him one day when he was walking across the parade at Fort Steele and killed him."

Amen Brown stood up on the other side of the fire, his hands moving nervously up and down his pants' legs. "What are you trying to say, Joe? You think we're going to get killed tomorrow?"

"Maybe tomorrow," Curly Joe said. "Or the day after tomorrow. All I'm trying to say is that if you're going to get a Ute bullet, you're going to get it, and there's no sense in trying to run away from it. You read the Bible. Why do you fear death?"

"I dunno," Brown admitted. "I've asked myself that a hundred times, but I never got an answer. All I know is that I don't want to die. There's too much to be done yet."

"You've had forty years of living," Curly Joe said. "What have you done with it?"

"Nothing," Brown said. "That's why I ain't ready to die."

He looked at Curly Joe and asked scornfully, "I suppose you are ready?"

"Why, yes," Curly Joe said. "I am."

"This is a hell of a stupid conversation," Lee said. "There's a chance we won't have any fighting and nobody will die."

"No," Curly Joe said with finality. "No chance at all. It will come tomorrow or the day after tomorrow, and some of us will die."

Lee threw up his hands. "How do you know so much about what's going to happen?"

"Don't ask me how I know," Curly Joe said. "I just know."

The man believed it, Lee thought. He didn't feel that it was his place to tell them what Thornburgh had decided. Besides, the situation was tricky because it was tense, and no one could know for sure what would happen—no one except perhaps Curly Joe Horn.

Lee glanced at Billy, who was watching him with narrowed eyes, his sharp-featured face very grim. Lee turned away, saying he'd better get some sleep. Billy was thinking of Melissa, Lee thought, and of what he had told the boy about looking out for her if anything happened to him. He had not, he decided, really removed the small worry at all.

Chapter 14

ON SUNDAY Thornburgh's command left Williams Fork and moved ten miles up Deer Creek to camp near its head. The column was now thirty-five miles from the Agency, but it was the toughest part of the march because nearly all of it was on the reservation, and several miles of it went through Coal Creek Canyon, which was as perfect a spot for an ambush as any Indian could dream up.

Lee Starbuck, reconnoitering ahead of the soldiers, realized that he and Joe Rankin were the only men in the expedition who fully understood the situation. Before he left that morning, he had sensed a growing nervousness among both the officers and men. He was not sure whether this was due to something Rankin had said, or because the column was so close to the reservation line. Or—and he knew this was a strong possibility—it could have been because Curly Joe Horn's prophecy had spread through the column, that the fight would come today or tomorrow and some would die.

Lee had no greater faith in Curly Joe's prophecies now than he'd had at first, but the facts were such that the man could be right. Lee had taken the scout job for one reason only: he had thought there was a chance the fight could be averted. Now he was doubtful that it could, but he was committed.

If Thornburgh led his command down Coal Creek Canyon, Lee would die along with Billy Buckles and Curly Joe Horn and the rest. It would be a miracle if anyone survived to tell the world that Curly Joe had been one of the most accurate prophets in the history of mankind.

Late in the afternoon Lee rode into camp to report to Thornburgh that he had seen a few Utes at a distance, but that he had discovered nothing to indicate that a fight was shaping up. Then he asked if the plan that had been agreed upon the night before was still in effect.

Thornburgh was silent a moment as he chewed on his cigar, then he said, "Yes, but we've had some bad news. Did you see the Gordon freight outfit?"

Lee nodded. "They're just ahead of us."

"Well, one of Gordon's bullwhackers came in while ago. He'd just talked to Colorow, who told him that the Indians would start shooting the minute we cross Milk Creek. It seems that both Jack's and Douglas's bands war-danced last night and they've sent their women and children south toward the Grand, about ninety lodges."

"We'd better stay on this side of Milk Creek," Lee said. "Whatever we do is a gamble, but I'm sure of one thing: Colorow meant it when he said they'd start shooting if we cross Milk Creek. If they do, Meeker and his people will die."

Captain Payne was standing behind Thornburgh listening. Now he said, "You want us to stop because we're afraid of a bunch of damned savages?" He shook his head. "We're here to settle this thing, and that's what we'll do."

"Captain," Lee said, meeting Payne's stare, "I suppose General Custer thought he was settling something. If that is the kind of settlement you want, you'll get it before you're out of Coal Creek Canyon." He turned to Thornburgh. "Major,

I think the biggest danger of a fight starting in a tight situation like this is from an accident. I'm dead sure that Jack won't order his men to fire unless you do."

"We won't," Thornburgh said quickly. "My orders are plain enough on the matter, but I don't see what we can do to stop a fight from starting by accident."

"Leave the column at Milk Creek and let me go with you to the Agency," Lee said. "I tell you I can talk to Jack. I think I can persuade him to hold his men back from the boundary. That'll go a long ways to prevent an accident from happening."

"Sir, I still consider it a mistake for you to go in with a small detail," Payne said to Thornburgh. "These bastards are treacherous. They'll murder you just as quickly as the Modocs murdered Canby."

Thornburgh dismissed Payne's worries with a quick gesture. He said, "I'm not Canby, and these Indians aren't Modocs." He studied Lee a moment, then he went on, "The trouble is we are plagued by uncertainty, Starbuck. If we were on the plains and were approaching a band of hostile Sioux or Cheyennes, we'd know we were headed into a fight and we'd know how to fight, but we don't know a damned thing about what the Utes will do. What's more, I doubt that you do."

"I know just one thing," Lee said quickly. "They'll fight if they're pushed. I've told you that right along."

"If this was twenty years ago, I'd agree with you," Thornburgh said, "but these Indians haven't done any fighting since then to speak of. They used to whip the tail off the Plains tribes, at least they would if they caught them in the mountains where we are; but now?" He shook his head, perplexed. "Sometimes I think the proper course for us to take tomorrow would be to march straight through to the Agency."

"If they were southern Utes," Lee said, "that would be the right thing to do. Or even if they were the Uncompahgres with Ouray giving the orders; but you're going up against the White River Utes. Ouray couldn't handle them even if he was here. They're living with the Old People. As far as they're concerned, you *are* back twenty years ago."

Captain Payne laughed. "That's absurd. These Indians have been to Rawlins. They've been over into Middle Park and North Park. Some of them have been to Denver. This is 1879, Starbuck, not '59."

"As far as these Indians are concerned, this *is* '59," Lee said, and he turned to his horse and mounted.

As he rode away, he wondered if Ma Frazer had taken the girls to Steamboat Springs yet. He wished he knew; he wished he had never listened to Billy Buckles, but had stayed on the Bear to look out for Melissa. A sense of failure swept over him as he thought there was nothing he could say or do that would prevent a fight; that it was as inevitable as the sunset, which was no more than an hour or two away. Curly Joe Horn did not have second sight. He simply had a coldly logical mind, and he, Lee Starbuck, had grabbed at a very small straw when he had taken this job in the hopes of preventing a war.

He found Curly Joe alone by the fire. He staked out his horse and dropped down beside the soldier, more tired than he had ever been in his life, though he didn't know why. Physically, it had not been a hard day.

"The fight didn't come today," Curly Joe said. "It will come tomorrow."

"How do you know?"

"Because it didn't come today."

Lee filled his pipe and lighted it with a burning twig, resistance building in him to Curly Joe's prophetic certainty. "No man can be so God-damned sure about something that ain't happened yet," he said almost angrily. "I don't believe a word of the hogwash Billy puts out about you having second sight. You're a smart man, but that's all you are."

Curly Joe considered that a moment, then he murmured, "No, Mr. Starbuck, I'm not even a very smart man. Remember I never made any claim to having second sight, but I do know that if we pour enough coal oil around us, some fool will toss a match into it."

Lee pulled on his pipe a moment, then he said, "I guess that's what worries me. We've tightened this business until it squeaks. All we need now is for somebody to pull the trigger. I was afraid finding Adam Simms's body would be enough."

"It might have been if you hadn't found out the truth about who killed him." Curly Joe leaned forward, the gentle smile tugging at the corners of his mouth. "Mr. Starbuck, let's play a game of supposing. We'll put into your hand the ultimate weapon. I don't know what it is, but as long as we're playing a game, we'll play a big one. Let's say this weapon will destroy not only your enemy but half of mankind as well. And right in front of you is Jack, who has a similar weapon in his hand. Both of you know what this weapon

71

will do. Now here is my question: Will you use that weapon on Jack, or will you stand there forever, knowing it's a draw?"

"I wouldn't stand there forever," Lee said, "but I wouldn't use it, either, if I knew it was that powerful."

"So you don't think you would use it," Curly Joe said, still smiling. "But suppose Jack makes a threatening move as if he's about to use his weapon and you think that if you use yours fast enough, you'll catch him flat-footed and you'll get him before he can get you."

"In that case I suppose I'd use it," Lee said reluctantly.

"Of course you would," Curly Joe said. "Or he would. That's the story of mankind. Maybe we never really intend to kill a lot of people, but that's what we do in the end. We're driven to it by fear, or maybe by our idea of self-preservation."

Later, after Billy and Amen Brown came to the fire, they cooked supper and watched the sun die in a final golden surge of glory. Gradually the great peaks to the east, Sleepy Cat and the distant Flattops, were lost in the failing light.

For a time the four of them sat around the fire, none feeling like talking. There was little conversation and no jubilation among any of the men. All of them, Lee thought, felt the tension; all of them sensed that tomorrow they would cross the reservation line, and what was to come would come.

Later, when Lee lay with his head on his saddle and stared at the sky with its thousand twinkling eyes, he thought of Melissa. Then, in spite of himself, his mind turned to Curly Joe's preposterous game of supposing about the ultimate weapon. He sighed, and just before he dropped off to sleep he thought that it was a good thing man wasn't smart enough to make such a weapon.

Chapter 15

PRIVATE BILLY BUCKLES stood guard that Sunday night through the dark hours, every sound magnified by his imagination until he was certain that Ute warriors were crawling through the sagebrush and were waiting until his back was turned to drive a knife between his shoulder blades. Every hoot of an owl, every coyote call, was a Ute signal.

Horses kicked and squealed on the picket line, and a trooper cursed them and told them to quiet down. The fires died down, until there was nothing left but smoldering coals dimly lighting the motionless figures of the sleeping cavalrymen. Or were they sleeping? Were they lying there motionless pretending to be asleep, while all the time they were thinking of tomorrow when they would reach Milk Creek and of the attack that would come—and some of them would die just as Curly Joe Horn prophesied?

Billy tried to remember how it had been when he was a boy, before his mother died. She would spend hours in the kitchen baking cookies and he would stay close to her like a hungry pup until she scolded him for being underfoot. Then, sorry that she had been sharp with him, she would pour a glass of milk from the crock in the pantry and tell him to take it along with a handful of cookies to the back yard and sit in the grass under a shade tree and have a picnic of his own.

He tried to think how it had been just before he'd left home, when he'd spent so much time with Lucy Monroe walking through the twilight and holding her hand, of kissing her as they stood in the darkness outside her house and of Lucy telling him she would always love him, no matter where he was.

He tried to think how it had been after he'd joined Company E, and how he hated the incessant drill and the fights that he couldn't avoid, or maybe didn't want to avoid because he had to prove to himself he was enough man to belong to Company E. He thought of the steady wind that swept across the parade and slapped the ropes against the flagpole and pelted the walls of the barracks with sand.

But nothing really came clear; he was listening for any sound that was strange, no matter how slight it was, or for the sight of a shadowy figure slipping toward him from out there in the night. Twice he almost pulled the trigger because he heard a faint rustling as some slithering night animal darted through the sagebrush. On both occasions he caught himself in time.

At dawn Curly Joe Horn built up the fire. They ate breakfast before the sun was up, the air sharp with its predawn chill. Lee Starbuck was grave and short-tempered for some reason that was beyond Billy.

73

Again his thoughts went back, this time to the summer he had worked for Lee, and with the memory was the knowledge that he had liked and admired the big rancher more than any other man he had ever known. Melissa was in his mind, too, the tall girl with the sweet lips and firm breasts and proud carriage, a girl so tall that he'd had to stand on his tiptoes to kiss her . . . . If he had only told her that summer that he loved her. . . .

If Lee Starbuck was out of the way, then he, Billy Buckles, would have to look out for her, just as Lee had told him to. Maybe a Ute bullet would find Lee today; or if it didn't, Billy would have his chance and no one would ever know who had fired the fatal shot.

One moment Billy thought he couldn't do it, the next he told himself he could. He knew at last what he wanted, but Lee's big body with its wide shoulders and strong arms stood between him and Melissa, Lee who had a way of managing life and making it give him what he wanted.

Billy hovered over the fire, shivering; then the pendulum swung again and he knew he couldn't do it. He had no talent for managing life. He wasn't Lee Starbuck; he was Billy Buckles, the smallest man in the company, who had to fight to prove he was a man, and all the time he wasn't really sure himself how good a man he was. He didn't even know how well he would stand up today when the shooting started. He was just little Billy Buckles who always arrived at his destination too late to get what he wanted.

Suddenly he was aware of Lee talking to Amen Brown and Curly Joe. "They called me in last night, though I don't know why, because they'd made up their minds and they wouldn't listen to me. The Major's going on to the Agency with a small detail. That'll include me. The rest of the column will camp on Milk Creek till dark, then it'll go over the Pass and down Coal Creek Canyon and be on top of Jack before he knows it."

"What's the matter with that?" Amen Brown said. "Seems to me Jack wouldn't raise a hand if he knew we were looking down the barrels of our Springfields at him."

"What's the matter with it?" Lee repeated, and he stared hard at the soldier. "It's not honest, that's what. We do a hell of a lot of talking about how the Indians break their word, but we break ours whenever it suits us. We've sent word that the column will camp on Milk Creek or thereabouts, and the Major will go on in with five men."

"I'd say the Major was smart," Amen Brown said. He sounded as if he thought Lee was an impractical dreamer. "We won't accomplish anything getting ourselves killed."

"You see, Mr. Starbuck, we all want to live." Curly Joe smiled. "This is true from Major Thornburgh and Captain Payne on down to us privates and the civilians who are with the column. If trickery is necessary to live, then we'll resort to trickery."

"Oh, hell!" Lee said in disgust.

He looked at Billy, and Billy, glancing away, felt the back of his neck burn as he wondered if Lee had read his mind and knew the poison that was in it. There was something in that level stare that made Billy think Lee was weighing him in the balances of his mind, and Billy knew he was coming up short.

"Isn't it true?" Curly Joe asked.

Lee swung around to look at Curly Joe. "I had a notion you didn't care much about living."

"I don't," Curly Joe said, "but I'm different."

"He sure as hell is," Amen Brown agreed.

Billy didn't say a word. He was scared, but he didn't want anyone to know it and he had a feeling all three of them did. He wasn't particularly scared of being shot and suffering, or even of dying, although that was bad enough and he wanted to live. He was afraid of not holding up his end when the time came, of breaking and running and showing everyone he was afraid. Just for once he wanted to be somebody else than little Billy Buckles who always got there too late.

They moved out before the sun drove the night chill from the air, Thornburgh signaling, "Forward, at a walk." Presently they were over the divide and had reached Milk Creek. The valley ran a good five miles in a southwesterly direction. Sagebrush was all around them, making the air pungent with its tangy scent. There was rabbit brush too, and cedar and piñons on the higher ridges.

From the top of the divide there was still no sign of Indians. Amen Brown said in a low voice, "We've had hell scared out of us without no good reason. This is Milk Creek and there ain't an Injun in sight."

"There will be," Curly Joe said.

They went on, following the Agency road that more or less paralleled the creek. Once Billy glanced back to the wagons that were far in the rear and saw the dust clouding the morning air, then he lifted his head to study the ridge lines above him. Still no Indians were in sight, a fact that did not prevent an icy prickle from darting along his spine. If they were going to camp on Milk Creek while Thornburgh went on with a small detail, they'd better be doing it or it would be too late.

They kept moving, passing Gordon's freight outfit and crossing the creek a number of times. When they reached a straight stretch in the road, they stopped to water the horses. Lee and Rankin had been scouting far ahead of the column. Now they returned to talk to Thornburgh. Presently Lieutenant Cherry rode back, bringing an order to Captain Lawson for Company E to move to the head of the column.

"We're the fighting Company E," Curly Joe said as if pleased.

"Yeah, we're a fine bunch of heroes," Amen Brown grumbled.

Thornburgh was still conferring with Captain Payne, Rankin, and Lee, and it was plain to Billy that Lee was not agreeing with the Major's decision. From the bits of conversation that Billy heard, he judged that the argument had something to do with water. Milk Creek was too low to water so many horses and mules; and Lee, who had been over the ground a week before, said the nearest adequate water supply was at Beaver Springs, which was five miles inside the reservation. They'd have to go that far, Thornburgh decided, and this, Billy knew, would be the point Lee was arguing against.

They moved on again, Thornburgh and Captain Lawson riding together at the head of the column. Lee and Rankin, along with Lieutenant Cherry, were scouting on ahead again, but Billy, seeing Lee's tall, straight figure in the saddle, thought that if Lee Starbuck died today with a Ute bullet in him, Billy Buckles would be to blame.

If Billy had not talked to Lawson about Lee, Lee would still be back on the Bear, or maybe taking Melissa to Steamboat Springs. He told himself he hated Lee, but knew at once that he did not; he knew, too, that he would rather Melissa would marry Lee than have her die at the hands of some Ute warrior. If Melissa died, her death, too, could be laid at his door.

Thornburgh signaled for the column to stop. Up ahead Lieutenant Cherry was motioning wildly, but for a moment his gestures meant nothing to Billy. Thornburgh was studying the ridge line through his field glasses.

"There they are, my friends," Curly Joe said. "If your eyes are good enough, you can see them. Some are on horses, some are on foot, and it is my guess that if a report is ever made of this affair it will say that we were attacked by more than a thousand painted, screaming savages."

Billy saw them then. He was sure there were not more than forty or fifty of them. He moistened his dust-caked lips as he glanced at Curly Joe. He asked, "Now what?"

"Why, we'll fight," Curly Joe said. "What else is there to do?"

Rankin was talking to Thornburgh, saying it was time to start shooting, but the Major shook his head. No, his orders were very plain on that point. He ordered Company E to move out off the trail to the right, and Payne's Company F to the left.

They waited then, the troopers staring at the Indians. Some of them waved their hats and a few of the Indians waved back. Lieutenant Cherry, who was up ahead, waved his hat. Amen Brown, seeing the Lieutenant's hat in the air and mistaking it for a signal to fire, yelled, "That's it." He raised his rifle and pulled the trigger.

Firing broke out all around Billy. Dust and powdersmoke swept in front of him and around him as horses whirled, and men yelled and cried out in agony as they were hit. In that short, chaotic moment Billy Buckles understood with sharp clarity what Curly Joe Horn had said one time, that a man cannot escape his destiny. He knew, too, that man, being given free will, shapes his destiny by the decisions he makes.

He, Private Billy Buckles, was here on Milk Creek with the other men of Company E, Third Cavalry, because of his own decision. He gave out a high yell and began firing, suddenly filled with a new and unexplainable joy.

No soft-bodied Lucy Monroe to hold hands with in the warm twilight, no band music to tap his feet to on the Fourth of July, no Judge Oscar Billington to stir him with patriotic oratory. These memories faded into some deep recess of his mind and were lost. There was only this moment; this was a test of a man, and he was not afraid.

Chapter 16

THIS DAY, Monday, September 29, 1879, was the longest day in Lee Starbuck's life. It started early for him, but the hours were especially long after 10 A.M., when Amen Brown fired the first shot. Along with Lieutenant Cherry and the others in the advance party, Lee worked his way back to Captain Payne's Company F. There he heard the bad news that Major Thornburgh had started back through the cottonwoods to help with the supply wagons in the rear, and had not been seen since. But someone had seen his riderless horse among the cottonwoods.

Payne was sitting down when Lee joined him. He had an arm wound that must have given him agony. And worries perhaps more painful than his wound were bothering him, Lee thought: the Major's apparent death; the nightmare of another Little Big Horn; the skill with which the Utes fought. They kept out of sight, they moved swiftly and silently, they were good shots, and, more than anything else, they were fighting with none of the fanfare and bluster that characterized a battle with the Plains tribes.

"We're trapped," Payne said to Lee as he struggled to his feet. "This makes your advice look good."

"We can hold out if we fort up," Lee said.

Payne nodded. "We'll pull back to the wagons. It's all we can do."

For the next few hours Lee had the feeling that hell could never be worse. The wagons had circled more than a hundred yards from the creek, the officers leaving a wide gap on the stream side that they had expected Gordon to fill, but Gordon's freight train had felt the quick and devastating attack, too, and he had left his wagons fifty yards away and with his men had joined the soldiers.

In spite of his wound and the weight of command that had suddenly fallen upon him, Payne did a good job bringing order out of the chaos that the Ute attack had brought about, a better job than Lee had expected him to do, suffering as he undoubtedly was. Payne ordered a pit dug in the middle of the enclosure for the wounded. Horses and mules were shot to fill the gap on the creek side of the circle. Boxes, barrels, sacks, and anything else that could be found were used to fill in under and around the wagons.

The Utes did not pour in upon the defenders, but seemed to be wraiths out there in the dust and smoke, and it was seldom that any of the soldiers or civilians in the circle had a clean target. All the time the Indians kept up a devastating fire that forced the men inside the circle to keep low.

Still, a group was able to work back through the cottonwoods to Lawson's Company E and bring them in. Lee volunteered to go, and he was relieved to find that Billy Buckles wasn't hurt. The boy was tired and was almost out of ammunition, but he was holding up.

Later, crouched inside the circle behind a dead horse, he told Lee there had been a few minutes when he didn't think any of them would reach the wagons. "They poured so much lead at us that you'd have thought they was using Gatling guns." He motioned to Curly Joe Horn. "He was right about it coming today and some of us getting killed."

"Too right," Lee said bitterly. "All of us should have known it."

Billy gripped his arm. "What about Melissa? You figure Ma took her to Steamboat Springs?"

"I wish I knew," Lee said. "I've been thinking about her ever since that first shot was fired." He looked at Billy. "Who fired it?"

Billy closed his dry, cracked lips, not answering for a moment; then he said, "Amen Brown."

"The fool!" Lee muttered. "The stupid fool!"

But, he thought, if Amen Brown hadn't panicked and fired, some other trooper would have. It had been written in the book from the beginning. Let a situation like this build up long enough, and sooner or later someone breaks under the pressure. Neither the soldiers nor the Indians wanted the battle, but they were having it just the same.

There was a lull until the middle of the afternoon, when a wind began blowing. The Utes built a fire in the grass and sage and a wall of flame rushed toward the wagon circle. Payne ordered a man to build a backfire, but it was a mistake, because the fire ran back toward the corral.

The wagon tops burst into flames and a wild scramble followed as the men beat them out. The Utes took advantage of the activity to start shooting again. Henrys, Winchesters, Ballards, Spencers, and Springfields exploded into deafening sound. By the time the fire had been put out, five more of Payne's men were dead.

Billy lay behind a dead horse, panting. He drew a sleeve across his forehead, and looked at Lee. "How do you figure our chances?"

"Good, if we can get some men through their lines who'll go for help."

Another lull in the firing and Billy said, "I wish I had a drink."

"There's water in the creek," Lee said. "Somebody's going to have to go after it."

Billy was silent again. Presently he asked, "You going for help?"

"If the Captain will take me."

"He will," Billy said. "You and Rankin both." He waited a moment, and added, "I want to go, too. I've got to know about Melissa."

"It's my guess the Captain will be looking for volunteers," Lee said.

"Lee, you . . ." Billy sat up and wiped his face again. "Lee, you know what I've thought about doing after I heard that you and Melissa are getting married?"

"I know," Lee said. "I knew Friday when you came to get me."

"You didn't think I'd do it?"

Lee hesitated, staring past Billy at Curly Joe, who had a peephole between two dead horses and had slid the barrel of his Springfield through it. The man had been fearless all afternoon. Now Lee wondered if he not only was ready to die as he had said once to Amen Brown, but actually was seeking it.

Slowly he brought his gaze back to Billy. He had wanted a moment to think, for he had hoped to avoid giving a direct answer. Finally he said, "I didn't know."

"But you knew I might, and you didn't say or do nothing."

Billy bowed his head, his back pressed against the dead horse, and for a moment he seemed close to tears. He said, "Funny how a man starts thinking on a day like this. I've always been afraid I'd do something bad, like running because I couldn't help myself, or shooting you in the back, when all the time I knew you were the best damn man I ever met. Well, I've had bullets flying all around me today. Two of 'em went through my clothes and another one parted my hair, but I haven't done nothing bad. I don't know how many Indians I've killed. Maybe none, but I sure have tried. I guess I'm not afraid any more of being afraid."

Studying the boy's troubled face, Lee sensed that it had taken this day with its danger and death to make a man out of Billy Buckles. He said, "I'll tell the Captain you want to go."

"I wish you would." He stared at the carbine that lay across his lap. "Lee, I know you'll make Melissa a good husband. Better'n I would."

"I sure aim to try," Lee said, "if she's still alive."

He was staring at a column of smoke rising above the hills far to the southwest. He said, "They're burning the Agency. That must be what it is."

"Then Meeker's dead," Billy said. "All of this was for nothing."

Lee nodded. "That's about the size of it—but maybe it's not for nothing. When it's over, something will be done with this bunch of Utes. The Uncompahgres too, maybe, but we'll have peace on White River for sure. On the Bear, too."

This time the lull lasted until dusk, except for an occasional shot from an Army sharpshooter or from a Ute who glimpsed movement inside the corral. Most of the horses and mules were dead. Johnson had done much of the damage, Lee thought. He had seen the big medicine man shoot enough to know that he was the best marksman among the White River Utes.

Suddenly someone yelled, "They're coming."

Lee grabbed his Winchester and forced the barrel through the peephole he had made between two dead horses. He saw the moving figures in the sagebrush across the creek. He recognized one of them, a boy he had seen around the Agency who wasn't over fifteen. Probably the boys and young men were responsible for the fight; they were always the hard ones to control.

He aimed at the boy, who was ducking and dodging as he came toward the breastwork, but he could not pull the trigger. He fired at another Indian who was farther away, then he heard Billy's Springfield and saw the Indian boy drop.

The charge faded out. Lee had emptied his Winchester, and now he lay back and reloaded.

He remembered that the young Indian boy was a relative of Nevero, and he probably had been trying to prove that he was a man. Perhaps Nevero had refused to let the boy go with him; and then Lee wondered where the subchief and his band of renegades were. If they were prowling along the Bear, they would go after Caroline, and if the Frazer women were still on their place, Ma and Melissa would be killed and Caroline kidnapped.

He would leave when it was dark, he decided, whether Payne sent him through the Indian lines or not.

Then he heard Lieutenant Cherry call, "Starbuck, the Captain wants to talk to you."

Chapter 17

LEE FOUND Captain Payne lying in a pit, his back against the bank, his face pale in the gathering dusk. Rankin and a corporal squatted in front of him, Lieutenant Cherry at his side.

"If you're looking for volunteers to go for help," Lee said, "I'm your man. So is Private Billy Buckles of Company E. He's small enough so he won't wear a horse down. He worked for me last summer and knows the country."

"Good." Payne motioned toward the corporal. "George Moquin from Company F has volunteered. Four will be all we'll send." He nodded at Lee. "Bring Buckles here."

Payne leaned his head back and closed his eyes until Lee returned with Billy. Then he said wearily, "Before any of you start tonight, you'd better know what you're up against. Starbuck, you seem to know these Utes better than anyone else does. What will happen if they catch you?"

"They'll castrate us, same as the Plains Indians would," Lee said. "Chances are they'd be about the same as Apaches when it comes to killing. It would be slow and hurt like hell. We'd all wish we could get it quick and easy."

Payne turned to Rankin. "Joe, what do you figure your chances are of getting through to Rawlins?"

"Good," Rankin said. "I can get grub and a change of

horses at Fortification Creek, and I can do it again at Baggs's spread on the Little Snake. I'll be in Rawlins sometime early Wednesday morning."

It was more of the man's bragging, Lee thought, and he couldn't keep from saying, "That'll be a hell of a good job of riding, Joe."

"I'll do it," Rankin said, and from his tone Lee almost believed him.

"All right," Payne said. "I want all of you to know how serious our situation is. Ninety-six men are in good shape, which means that forty-six are dead or wounded. We've got about fifty horses and mules left, maybe less by now, and if we wait much longer we won't have any. Our rations will last until Thursday or Friday. After that we'll be eating horse meat, and it'll be so rotten we'll have a hard time getting it down. We'll probably be sick if we do. All I'm saying, gentlemen, is that if you don't get help to us within the next five or six days, we'll die here."

"I'll make it," Rankin said.

"You'll wait until after ten before you move out," Payne said. "It will be as dark then as it's going to be any time during the night. I will dictate a message to Lieutenant Cherry for Joe, who will wire it from Rawlins to General Crook. I will give Corporal Moquin a message to deliver to Lieutenant Price at Fortification Creek. Private Buckles will be with Corporal Moquin. Starbuck, I'll give you one to hand to Captain Dodge, who might be in Middle Park or somewhere on the Gore Pass road. Maybe on Bear River. I don't know. Just find him."

He paused a moment, fighting his pain and weariness, then he went on, "Joe will lead you up Milk Creek and over the divide. If you run into any Indians, Joe goes on. The other three will do all you can to hold the Indians off so Joe can get through. Do you understand?"

"Yes, sir," Billy said, and Moquin nodded.

"I understand, all right," Lee said, "but if there are any settlers left on Bear River, they'll be in danger. I've said all along that Nevero and his bunch won't have much stomach to fight us, but they'll raise hell with the settlers."

"All right, warn the settlers," Payne said, "but find Dodge. He's the closest help we can look for, and by this time I think the settlers are in Steamboat Springs or Rawlins."

Lee doubted that, but he didn't argue with Payne. None of the settlers, Ma Frazer or any of them, should be home.

All of them knew how the situation was shaping up, but many were as stubborn as Ma Frazer and might not leave their homes until news of the fighting reached them. All Lee could hope for was that he would be able to make a quick contact with Captain Dodge and then be free to ride down-river and warn anyone who had remained on his claim.

"Sir," Billy said, "if we reach Fortification Creek, we'll be out of the Indians' reach. I understand that I am to stay with Corporal Moquin that far, but I'd like your permission to return to Bear River after we reach Fortification Creek. Some of the settlers are my friends and I'd like to warn them, in case Lee goes on to Middle Park to find Captain Dodge."

Payne raised a hand and rubbed his face as he thought about it, then he asked, "Joe, is that right, that you'll be safe once you reach our supply depot on Fortification Creek?"

"I think so," Rankin said. "Nevero don't have no big bunch, not enough to raid on north. I'd say he'll hit Bear Valley and then swing back here."

Payne turned his head to look at Billy. "Permission granted," he said.

"Thank you, sir," Billy said.

"I'll excuse you now to do whatever needs to be done before you start," Payne said.

Lee and Billy returned to their position behind the breast-work of horses. They were silent a long time until Billy said, "We ain't heard any racket for a spell. No shooting or nothing. You reckon they're gone?"

"No," Lee said. "They're out there, all right. The best we can hope for is that they aren't on the creek or north along the road the way we've got to go. I think there's a good chance they won't be. They are a lot like children sometimes. Don't seem to look ahead."

Word that they were going had spread along the line and some of the men, including Curly Joe, came to them and shook hands and wished them luck. Curly Joe remained after the others had gone.

"If you've got second sight," Billy said, "I wish you'd tell me whether we're going to make it or not."

"I never told anybody I had second sight," Curly Joe said. "That was Amen Brown's idea, but you'll make it. If you ask me how I know, I'll tell you. I have confidence in you." He paused, then added, "You remember when I told you that the fears of men are many, that man is afraid to live and he's more afraid to die?"

"I remember," Billy said, "but I was afraid of something else."

"I know," Curly Joe said, "but you're not now, are you?"

"Not after this morning," Billy said. "Funny what can happen to a man in a few hours. I'll never be afraid again— not the way I used to be."

"But what changes a man one way will turn another man the opposite direction," Curly Joe said. "I'm thinking about Amen. He knows what he did when he fired that shot this morning. Now he's in kind of a stupor. Maybe you ought to talk to him."

But nothing that either Billy or Lee said got through to the man. He sat with his back against a dead horse, his Springfield on the ground beside him, his glassy eyes staring into space. Presently Curly Joe said, "It's no use. It isn't God who judges us. We judge ourselves, and Amen has condemned himself to hell."

Lieutenant Cherry crossed the enclosure to them and said it was time to move out. A few minutes later they followed Rankin out of the circle to the creek, and then they turned upstream, Rankin still leading.

Lee expected gunfire to break out every minute; he rode with every muscle tense, the thought possessing him that he might hear the shooting and feel the hot, probing passage of a bullet, or he might hear nothing at all. But he heard no sound except the soft thud of hoofs against the hard dirt of the road and the grunting and heaving of the horses as they labored over the divide.

No shot was fired, no Ute yell came to break the night silence, and to Lee's way of thinking a miracle had been achieved. Once out of the valley, they had a good chance of making it. He sensed the relief that was in the others, and a moment later Rankin quickened the pace.

Chapter 18

AFTER the four couriers left, Curly Joe Horn lay beside the motionless Amen Brown listening for the gunfire that would mean the Utes had discovered the four riders. Brown was still in a stupor and seemed unaware of anything that went on around him. Besides Brown, only the dead and the wounded who were unconscious did not realize how important these minutes were.

Curly Joe, along with the other soldiers and the civilians, remained quiet and listened. No one talked. For a time it seemed that even the wounded hushed their groans. The minutes passed until an hour had gone by; then Sergeant O'Brien said, "They must have made it. We'd have heard the shooting by now if they hadn't."

Curly Joe knew the silence was no assurance of life for them. Even with the best of luck, five or six days would pass before help would come. Thornburgh was dead. Payne and most of the officers were wounded. All that the able-bodied could do was to stay inside the wagon circle and repel the attacks that were sure to come. They could not fight their way clear and leave the forty-odd wounded to die helplessly under the guns and knives of the Utes.

There was no shade, and even in late September the days might be hot. There would not be enough water, even though brave men would take the risk and go to the creek and return with water if they were able to. Supplies would be gone in a few days. The stench of death and the stink of rotting carcasses would be all around them, and there would be no escape.

If the survivors stayed alive and retained their sanity, they had no guarantee that the couriers would bring help, even though they succeeded in threading their way through the Ute lines. Small bands of Utes would be wandering around to the north along Williams Fork or Bear River.

Curly Joe remembered what Lee Starbuck had said about Nevero being the kind of renegade who would not stay here and fight, but would be looking for easier victims than soldiers forted up in a corral of wagons and dead horses. If the couriers ran into one of these bands, they could die as easily on Williams Fork or Bear River as they could right here on Milk Creek.

He felt Amen Brown stir beside him, and a moment later he heard him ask, "Where are we?"

"On Milk Creek," Curly Joe said. "We're forted up in a circle, and four men have gone for help."

Brown was coming out of his stupor, and he began to curse. "I remember. I saw the Lieutenant wave his hat and I thought we was supposed to fire, and I did, and God damn it, I started the war."

He got to his feet, his Springfield in his hand. "Sit down," Curly Joe said.

"The hell I will!" Brown shouted. "I'm going out there and kill every Indian there is."

Curly Joe grabbed the man by the waistband and brought him tumbling down as Sergeant O'Brien rushed toward them and demanded to know what the ruckus was about.

"Brown was going out there and kill all the Utes who are holding us down," Curly Joe said.

"Is he now?" O'Brien said angrily. "Has he lost the little sense the good God gave him?"

"It seems that he has," Curly Joe said. "He fired the first shot and started the whole shebang and he blames himself. Just now he came to and started remembering."

Brown leaned against a dead horse and babbled something about killing all the Indians who were hiding in the darkness. O'Brien swore and picked up Brown's Springfield. "He's always been a good soldier, but you never know what's going to happen to a man when the guns go off. I've seen better men than Brown go daft. Keep him inside, Horn. Right now he's dangerous. I'll take his Springfield until he gets over it."

"I'll try, Sergeant," Curly Joe said.

Amen Brown was silent after O'Brien left. Perhaps he had dropped off to sleep—Curly Joe wasn't sure. In any case, it was better to leave him alone as long as he was quiet. Curly Joe thought about Billy Buckles and Amen Brown and some of the others giving him credit for having second sight. The whole thing had started with a few good guesses, and after that it had become a sort of game. Only Lee Starbuck had come right out and said he didn't believe it. A good man, this Starbuck, honest and outspoken and possessing a compassion even for Indians.

But how could any white man have compassion for Indians? Curly Joe rubbed his forehead, suddenly sick as memories swept through his mind, memories he had kept bottled up for years. When they had at times broken through into his consciousness, he had got drunk or gone to the post hospital with a fever, or worked up a fight with anyone who was near him.

Now he could do none of these things, and for the first time in ten years he didn't want to. He sat there with his fists closed and sweat pouring down his face. He had refused to remember; he had built a wall around those terrible hours on the Solomon River in Kansas.

In a way he was like Amen Brown. Not that he had the guilt feeling that Brown had. He had forgotten because he had to, because the memory had been too painful to recall. He did remember he had wanted to die. For ten years he had wanted to die, but here he was, alive and not even injured, when men like Major Thornburgh were dead and Captain Payne wounded.

Yes, he remembered, and for a time he lived those hours again. He had been living with his parents in a sod house on the Solomon expecting to go away to college in the fall. He had married a neighbor girl named Nora, small, but vital and strong, as perfect a wife as a man could have. He planned to be a preacher. He studied the Bible every night, and during the day he often talked to his neighbors who had not been saved, trying to convert them and save them from the torments of hell.

Then the Cheyennes came up from the south and attacked the Solomon Valley settlers without warning. They hit the Horn place at dawn just as he was leaving the sod house with his father to milk. His father was killed, and he was hit by a bullet that gave him a scalp wound and knocked him cold. The Cheyennes lifted a patch of hair and left him for dead, and after killing his mother and Nora, they rode on.

When he came to, the pain in his head was so great that he fainted when he got to his feet and fell across his father's body. When he came to the second time he staggered to his feet and reached the door of the sod house. Blood had run down his forehead into his eyes and had dried there so that he had to dig it out with his fingers before he could see.

He clutched the door casing, staring at his mother, who lay in a pool of blood; then slowly his gaze turned to Nora in the far corner of the room, her head split open, an arm lying ten feet from her body. He fainted again.

This time he did not regain consciousness until some neighbors came and put him in a wagon and took him to their house and nursed him back to life. Not to health, for nothing was ever really right after the day of the raid. He recovered his strength and went away and joined the Army. That had been his life ever since.

For the first time in ten years he felt as if he wanted to live, as if the memory of that bloody day had gripped his mind and squeezed it dry and now had been washed away. He could think about what had happened without the usual pain in the top of his head that felt as if it were about to explode, without the compulsion that had always driven him into a world of forgetfulness or of sodden drunkenness, or to a hospital bed to lie for days with a consuming fever or the red, blazing madness that had driven him to seek a fight.

For the first time in all these years he wanted to live. It seemed to him that suddenly his mind was filled with wisdom, and he understood how a man like Lee Starbuck could have compassion for the Utes. He was that big a man; he knew that they had been driven to do what they had. Now he, Curly Joe Horn, realized that the Cheyennes too had been driven to do what they had done.

Life was made up of opposites. Good and evil. God and the devil. Black and white. Heat and cold. Love and hate. White men and red men. Sorrow and happiness. Day and night. The strong and the weak.

Everything must be kept in balance; there had to be a cause for every effect. Not that he understood what they were. Probably he never would, but at least he had been given this tiny capsule of wisdom. It was big enough to make him aware that no sane man seeks death, that life is the greatest of all gifts, and he realized that he had not used his to the best of his ability.

When he thought about the Army years, he knew why he had sought refuge in the other world that Billy Buckles and Amen Brown used to talk about, a world in which he could shut off the flow of foolish words that other men said to him. All words were foolish, and he knew that what he had done, the way he had lived, was wrong. He had more to give than the equally foolish words he had spoken to Billy and Amen Brown and the others, something of the strength and courage he had seen in Lee Starbuck.

He heard Brown cry out in his sleep for water. "I'll go after some," Curly Joe said, and picked up the canteens.

Gripping his Springfield in his right hand, he slid over the horse barricade and worked his way to the creek. He filled the canteens and stopped to listen. It was almost dawn now; a new day was at hand. More fighting and shooting and dying would come with it, he thought, and he started back toward the wagon circle.

He did not hear the big Indian move toward him, or see him until it was too late. The Ute's knife slashed downward, ripping open the front of his body from his heart through his stomach and into his belly. He fired the Springfield, and in a strange and unfamiliar light that illuminated the whole scene for no more than a second, he saw that he had drilled a hole through the Ute's head.

He fell across the two canteens he had dropped, the blood that spurted from the gaping wound covering them. A last thought crossed his mind: that everything must be kept in balance by opposites, life and death, and this was death.

Then he was spinning and spinning and spinning far out into space. This, he knew, was the journey from which there was no return.

Chapter 19

LEE left the others at Williams Fork and angled northeast. It was dark, and the sky still showed no sign of dawn. He was slowed by the rough country and by a sudden, violent storm, so that it was Wednesday morning when he rode into the tiny settlement of Hayden. He was surprised to find Captain Safford Dodge and his company of Negro cavalrymen there ahead of him.

Lee told Dodge about the supply depot on Fortification Creek and about what had happened, and he reported that Joe Rankin and two soldiers were riding north, Rankin to go on to Rawlins to wire Crook about the fight on Milk Creek.

Lee remained in Hayden long enough to eat dinner. He asked if the Frazer women had gone through the settlement on their way to Steamboat Springs. No one had seen them, although several families from the lower valley had either stopped at Hayden or had gone upstream to the bigger settlement of Steamboat Springs.

He left Hayden ahead of Dodge and his troopers, condemning himself for taking the job with Thornburgh's expedition. If he had stayed on the Bear, he and Melissa would have been in Steamboat Springs before a shot was fired on Milk Creek, but he had made the mistake of believing that Ma would keep her promise. He was sure she hadn't, because the people at Hayden had been on the alert, keeping at least one guard out all the time. It would not have been possible for three women to ride through the settlement without being seen.

Dodge and his company had come in from their camp near Gore Pass by way of Twenty-mile Park. They had not seen any Indians, and the people in Hayden hadn't either. Neither fact meant that Nevero wasn't in the vicinity. He was like a coyote sneaking into a farmer's chicken house. The chances were good that he'd have his chicken and be gone before the farmer knew it.

In Nevero's case the chicken was Caroline Frazer. He would not forget how Caroline had laughed at him when he had asked her to be his wife, or how Ma Frazer had run him off with a cocked shotgun.

The black gelding had covered too many miles since Lee had left Milk Creek to be hurried now. Lee rode slowly and rested the horse often, and it was well into afternoon by the time he came within sight of his buildings. They were still standing. That was more than he had expected, and it gave him hope.

He had not been able to think coherently after leaving Hayden. The fear that Melissa was dead pressed on his mind. Meeker's people had probably all died when the Agency buildings were burned. Thornburgh and a number of his men were dead, and more would die before the battle was over. It was hard to tell how many settlers would lose their lives before the Utes were brought under control.

These deaths were all parts of the tragedy that had begun on White River, but Melissa's death would be more than tragedy to Lee Starbuck. It would be the end of everything for him, the end of his dreams and plans, the end of a purpose in life that had been slow to come to him and end his drifting, rootless years.

Now for a moment he hoped, for he looked past his buildings to the Frazer house and barn and sheds, all standing exactly as they had the Friday afternoon he had left with Billy Buckles. That Friday seemed years ago, not the few days it had actually been. He had feared he would find only ashes here, and the mutilated bodies of Melissa and her mother.

But the hope flared only briefly and was gone when he was close enough to see that no smoke rose from the Frazer chimney. The afternoon was cool and they would surely need a fire. Besides, it was time to be starting supper. Something was wrong.

Then, in the way a drowning man reaches for any bit of

driftwood that could help, he wondered if they were hiding in the brush along the river. But that wouldn't be like Ma. Pa Frazer had put up those buildings. As she had often said, they were all that she had left of him, and she would fight and die for them if it came to that.

An involuntary shudder shook him as he pulled up in front of the Frazer house and stepped down. Hope was a candle flame that flared and almost died, and flared and almost died again; and then he heard her running steps and her cry, "Lee! Lee! Thank God you're alive!"

Melissa was carrying a shovel. She did not drop it until she threw out her arms to hug him. He kissed her lips that were salty with her tears, and held her a long time, her face pressed against his coat. Even with her trembling body against his, he found it hard to believe that she was alive and as vibrant and strong as ever.

She needed to cry, she wanted to, but she could not. She held him as if she, too, were afraid he was no more than a dream. When she finally stopped trembling, she said, her mouth against his coat so that her voice was muffled, "Ma's dead. I was digging her grave."

"What?" He pushed her away and stared at her pale, stricken face. "How did it happen?"

She didn't answer for a time, but took his hand and led him into the house and on through the front room to her mother's bedroom. Melissa had put her mother's good black dress on her and laid her out on the bed. Her hands were folded over her breast. Her eyes were closed, but her lips had sagged apart so that her mouth was partly open. Staring at her, Lee could see little resemblance to the big, hearty woman he had known.

He turned to Melissa and asked again, "How did it happen?"

She choked and turned away and walked back into the front room. There she sat down, staring at her hands that were gripped so tightly the knuckles were white. She said, "Lucky Boman shot and killed her Tuesday morning."

She swallowed, then she lifted her head to look at him. "I still can't believe it happened. You see, Caroline's been gone since Sunday. She didn't want to go to Steamboat Springs, you know, so Ma put it off, but Saturday night she told Caroline that all three of us were going Sunday morning, even if she had to tie Caroline and haul her there in the wagon.

"Some time during the night Caroline sneaked out. I don't

know what Ma really thought, but she told me the Indians had her. I said Caroline had gone to stay with Boman. Ma slapped me then and called me a liar. She tried to make me believe she thought Nevero had sneaked in through the window and carried Caroline off, but she couldn't have really thought it. I guess she'd shut her eyes to Caroline's orneriness so long that she couldn't admit even to me that Caroline would do anything bad.

"Ma wouldn't leave for Steamboat Springs without Caroline. She moped around the house and looked out of the window every few minutes. She didn't sleep any either night. Tuesday morning Boman rode up. I was in the barn and didn't know he was here till I heard a shot. I ran into the house and found Ma lying on the floor in the front room. A rifle was on the floor beside her.

"I heard a horse and looked out. Boman was riding off. Ma was shot in the chest and she didn't live long. She tried to talk, but she couldn't say much. As near as I could make out, Boman had come for Caroline's things and Ma got a rifle and tried to kill him. Maybe he shot her in self-defense, but just the same he killed her, and all because Caroline was too big a coward to come back herself."

Melissa stared at her hands and shook her head slowly. "I've thought about it ever since, Lee. It seems to me that Caroline killed her just as much as Boman did, even if he was the one who pulled the trigger."

"I'm sorry, Melissa," he said. "I'm more sorry than I can say. I thought a lot of Ma, too."

"We'd best bury her," she said tonelessly. "I've got the grave almost deep enough. Maybe you will finish it."

"Of course I will," he said.

She went with him when he left the house. He picked up the shovel and followed her to the unfinished grave that was a few feet from where her father was buried.

"I thought Ma would like to be buried close to Pa," Melissa said.

Neither of them said anything more until the grave was finished. Lee climbed out and said, "We don't have a coffin."

A sudden, uncontrollable chill struck her so that for a time she couldn't say anything. When she could speak, she said, "We'll wrap her in a blanket. Seems like she's got to be buried tonight. I was alone last night with her. I just couldn't stand it another night."

They went inside. Melissa found a blanket and brought it to Lee, who wrapped the body in it and carried it outside. Melissa followed with a Bible. Lee gently lowered the body into the grave and then took the Bible from Melissa. The light was fading rapidly but it was still strong enough for him to read the Twenty-third Psalm. He recited the Lord's Prayer from memory, then handed the Bible back to Melissa and filled the grave.

He hurried as fast as he could, but it was dark by the time he finished. As they walked to the house, Melissa said, "Let's go to your place, Lee. I can't stay here—I'll go crazy if I do. Last night I thought I heard Pa's voice telling me he never knew what kind of woman Caroline was when he was alive."

"All right, we'll go to my place," Lee said.

He went into the front room and struck a match. He saw that Melissa had replaced the rifle on the pegs near the door. He took it and went back to where Melissa waited beside his black gelding. He took the reins and, leading the horse, started toward his place, Melissa beside him.

As they walked, he listened for any sound that might warn him of the presence of Indians, but he heard nothing that alarmed him. Then he thought of Lucky Boman and Caroline, and wondered if she knew that Boman had killed her mother. Perhaps it was unfair, but the thought occurred to him that it wouldn't make any difference if she did know.

Chapter 20

THEY had supper at Lee's house, and Melissa was utterly worn out when she had finished the dishes. She said, "I don't know what's the matter with me, Lee. I've never felt this way before. I've always been strong, stronger even than Ma."

She turned away from him and added, her back to him, "I used to think I hated Ma because of the way she favored Caroline, but I didn't really. I depended on her more than I ever dreamed. Now I don't have anybody but you."

"You need some rest." He blew out the lamp and, leading her to the bed, held her in his arms as he said, "This is your home now, Melissa. I love you, and I'll try to make you happy. Please remember that."

"I will," she said. "If I hadn't been so sure that you loved me and that you would come back I would have gone crazy last night. I kept thinking how cold and stiff Ma's body was, and Caroline sleeping somewhere with Boman and not knowing or maybe not caring about him killing Ma. I can understand a little about why the Utes kill white people; but Boman . . ."

She began to cry, and she whispered, "Why does God let things like this happen, Lee? Why?"

"I don't know," he said. "I just don't know."

Presently she dropped off to sleep. He lay beside her, an arm around her, her head on his shoulder. He thought about her question and told himself that it had been asked from the beginning of time, or at least from the moment that the concept of a just and loving God had come to man. The question would never be answered, at least not to Melissa's satisfaction, and then he wondered what Curly Joe Horn would say if Melissa had asked him. He didn't know what answer Curly Joe would make, but the man would have one. Lee was sure of that.

He dropped off to sleep, and woke before dawn. Melissa, he thought, had not moved. Carefully he drew his arm away from her and eased off the bed. He pulled on his coat and, picking up the Winchester from where he had leaned it against the wall, opened the door, and slipped outside. If Nevero was in the valley and intended to make an attack, dawn would probably be the time.

He remained by the front door of the cabin as light began to show on the eastern horizon and seep across the sky. He stood there, shivering a little in the chill fall air and watching the mist rise from the river. He thought about Curly Joe, and remembered Billy Buckles telling him how the man seemed to live in two worlds, that on occasion he did not appear to hear what was said to him or even to know what was going on around him. A strange man, but not so strange after the firing started Monday morning. Then he had acted as if he had suddenly awakened from a long dream and now was fully alive.

Lee was conscious of an owl hooting from somewhere down the river. He moved away from the front door and stopped, not sure how far away the Indians were, but he guessed they were close to the Frazer house. He stood motionless, his heart pounding in great slugging beats.

He wondered how many Utes were in the party, and if they would attack and he would die here in his own cabin after surviving the first day of the fighting on Milk Creek and the ride out of the valley that night. Melissa would die if he did. It was a wonder she was still alive, a wonder that Boman had not hunted for her and killed her after shooting Ma Frazer. For he had left a witness who would hang him if he was ever brought to trial; but he must have panicked and not thought of Melissa being somewhere around the place.

He stepped back to the door, deciding that there was too much light to run the risk of the Indians catching a glimpse of him. Then he heard another owl hoot from a great distance down the river, and presently the faint beat of hoofs came to him, and was lost a moment later. They had pulled out. He thought about it, trying to decide what had drawn them off, but he could not make any sense out of it.

He stayed by the door and watched the new day being born. He wondered if Captain Payne and Lieutenant Cherry and Curly Joe and the rest were still alive. Had Captain Dodge reached them with his colored troopers, and were there enough of them to drive the Utes off? Had Rankin reached Rawlins and was a relief party on the way?

He had questions, but the answers would be slow coming. Gradually the morning light spread across the valley. The stars died and the sky turned blue, and presently in the east the sun came up, its rim showing above the Continental Divide, and its slanting, golden light striking the cottonwoods along the river.

All the time another question had been nagging him, and this one, he knew, must be answered. What was he going to do with Melissa while he hunted for Lucky Boman?

That he would hunt for Boman and find him and kill him was a foregone conclusion, but he couldn't take Melissa with him. He couldn't leave her alone, and he couldn't afford the time it would take to escort her to Steamboat Springs, or even to Hayden.

He went inside and built a fire. The slight noise he made woke Melissa and she sat up. He put the coffee pot on the stove, watching her, and for a moment he thought she did not remember what had happened and why she was here with him. He said, "Good morning, Melissa," and saw her face turn pale and her lips tighten. He knew then that she was remembering.

"Good morning, darling," she said, and came to him and kissed him. "I'll get breakfast in just a few minutes."

She went outside, and he turned toward a shelf and picked up a slab of bacon and began to slice it. He had not told her he was going after Boman, but he was sure she knew. She would have been disappointed in him if he didn't. By the time she came in again he had made his decision as to what he would do with her.

"Melissa, I guess you know I'm going after Boman," he said. "I don't know what I'll do with Caroline if I find her alive except put her on a train for Denver and forget her."

"It's what I intended to do if I found her," Melissa said. "I never want to live in the same house with her again."

"The way I figure it, they'll hit for Rawlins," Lee said. "I'm sure Boman killed Simms and took his money. We found Simms's body on Williams Fork. Boman tried to make it look as if the Utes had done it, but I know different. Now that the fight's started, he's not likely to find a buyer for the trading post, but he may drive his pony herd to Rawlins. If he does, I'll catch him between the trading post and Rawlins, and I'll probably find Caroline with him."

She was setting the table as she listened to him. Now she said, "I won't stay here."

"Of course not," Lee said. "I wouldn't let you. I thought you'd go with me as far as the supply depot on Fortification Creek. You'll be safe there while I'm hunting for Boman."

She whirled to face him, her expression one of wild rebellion. "Maybe I don't want to be safe," she cried. "Why should you take all the risks? If I'm to be your wife, I ought to take the same chances you do. You'll forget what Caroline is and turn your back to her and she'll kill you."

"No, she won't," he said. "If I've got her pegged right, she'll think she'll still need a man after Boman's dead, so all of a sudden she'll discover she loved me all the time."

Melissa nodded, her face dark with anger. "You're right. That's exactly what she'll do."

He decided not to tell her that Nevero's band or some other band of Utes had been nearby this morning. It would only worry her. He let her finish her breakfast, and then he said, "I'll saddle Blacky and fetch a horse for you. You want your buckskin?"

She nodded, and before he could leave the cabin she ran to him and put her arms around him. She said, "I've got to

97

go with you, Lee. I've got to know what is happening to you. You don't know how it's been since you left Friday."

"We'll see," he said gently. "Throw some grub into a sack. Enough for a couple of days."

She was ready by the time he returned, leading her buckskin. He helped her up, tied the sack of food behind his saddle, and mounted. They stopped at the Frazer house long enough for her to get a change of clothes, a revolver, and the money Ma had hidden under the floor; then they went on downstream.

Lee watched the brush along the river and the ridge lines on both sides of the valley, wondering how far the Indians had gone, or if they had gone at all. Presently he saw smoke ahead and guessed that Boman's trading post was burning. He wasn't sure what it meant. If Boman and Caroline had been inside when the Indians showed up, they very likely were dead—Boman at least. If it was Nevero's band, they wouldn't kill Caroline if they could help it.

Still, even with every sense alert, he was startled when Billy Buckles rode out of the brush along the river and waved to them. He watched Billy canter up, the expression on the boy's face telling him that Billy had been through a terrifying time.

Before Lee could say anything, Billy said in a tight voice that almost broke, "The Indians have got Caroline and Boman. I left the supply depot before sunup. Rankin went on ahead of us, then I rode with Moquin a while and when we'd gone far enough so it seemed like he was safe, I came back to the camp. It was when I was coming down here this morning that I seen the Indians. I got under cover before they spotted me or I wouldn't be alive. There was five of 'em. Caroline and Boman was driving a pony herd north when the Utes caught 'em. The Indians burned the post and crossed the river. I don't know where they went."

He swallowed hard, his gaze swinging from Lee to Melissa and back to Lee again; then he blurted, "If it had been some folks, I'd have done what I could to save their hair, but Boman ain't worth saving, and I figured Caroline wasn't much better."

He expected to be condemned, Lee thought; but most men, knowing Boman and Caroline, and with the odds five to one, would have done exactly what Billy had.

"No, they're not worth saving, for a fact," Lee said, "but I'm going after Boman just the same. He murdered Me-

98

lissa's mother, and there's a chance the Indians might not kill him."

"I'll go with you—" Billy began.

"No, you'll have to take Melissa to the supply depot," Lee said. "We can't leave her here alone and I can't take her with me."

Billy glanced quickly at Melissa to see if she seemed willing to go with him. She nodded gravely as she said, "I guess that's what we'd better do." Her gaze lingered on Lee's face a moment, then she said quietly, "Be careful, Lee. Please be careful."

He kissed her, and said, "I will. I've got to come back. We've got a life to live together."

He nodded at Billy, and rode on down the river to the first riffle. He crossed to the south bank, picked up the tracks of the Indians and their captives, and followed them into the hills.

As he rode he asked himself the question: Were these two people worth this risk, a man he had promised himself to kill and a woman who had caused as much trouble as Caroline had?

He told himself they weren't worth it at all. Still, he would rescue them from the Indians if he could. Boman should be executed for murder, but even a murderer should not have to endure the torture that Nevero would give him.

Later, near noon, he stopped at a small stream to water his black. The tracks were very clear here—three Indian ponies and the two horses Caroline and Boman were riding. Suddenly he remembered that Billy had said there had been five Utes. He went on, pondering this. He was not sure what it meant, but a sense of uneasiness grew in him until it was almost intolerable.

Chapter 21

PRIVATE BILLY BUCKLES swelled with pride as he rode beside Melissa. He glanced at her often, thinking she was beautiful even now, sad as she was about her mother and worn out as she must be.

"I'm sorry about your ma, Melissa," he said. "I'm awfully sorry."

"Thank you, Billy," she said, and kept her eyes on the long slope ahead of them.

She didn't want to talk—that was plain enough, and he could understand it. To Billy's way of thinking, Ma Frazer had not been a woman anybody could love. Not by Melissa anyway, after having been made a work horse the way she had been. But Ma had been big and strong and dependable, and she had kept her family together. Besides, she had been Melissa's mother, and Melissa was the kind of person who would grieve for her whether she had reason to or not.

He wondered how it had happened. Lucky Boman was strictly no good, and he had probably committed every crime there was, at one time or another, but he was smart, smart enough to know that killing a woman was the last thing he could do in this country and expect to live. No, something must have happened that had made him do it.

Billy opened his mouth to ask, but when he glanced at Melissa, he shut it without saying a word. She wasn't just grieving, he decided. Perhaps she wasn't thinking about her mother at all. She probably was thinking about Caroline maybe, or Lee.

The thought of Lee started the pride swelling in him again. Lee had known about the bad thoughts he'd had, thoughts that were really crazy. Even if he had removed Lee as a rival, he had no reason to think that Melissa would ever love him.

Well, he was finished with that craziness. It was enough to make a man proud to know that Lee trusted him and accepted him as an equal. He had told Captain Payne about him wanting to be a courier. Now he was trusting him with Melissa's life, and that was the most important thing in the world to Lee Starbuck.

He had accomplished it at last, Billy thought—he had proved he was a man. He had fought as well as anyone last Monday; he had killed at least one Indian when they made their charge in the afternoon. He had volunteered with the others Monday night and had kept up with them as they had ridden north.

He'd been scared, sure; but when it came down to that, he guessed the other three were scared, too. After he reached

100

the supply depot, he could have stayed there, but he had gone on with George Moquin for a time, and then he had ridden back to Bear River to find out if Melissa was alive and to warn any settlers who were still there.

No, he wasn't little Billy Buckles who always reached where he was going too late. Not any more. He hadn't broken and run when the bullets started flying or when the danger was all around him in the darkness as it had been when they had ridden out Monday night, the pressure squeezing his chest until he could hardly breathe. No, by God, he was a soldier, and he'd proved he was fit to belong to Company E.

He thought about the men pinned down inside the wagon circle back there on Milk Creek. He wondered if there had been any more attacks, and if Curly Joe Horn and Amen Brown and Sergeant Pat O'Brien were still alive. He'd always thought he hated O'Brien, who had bullied him time after time, but he didn't hate him now. He could even think of him with some liking. The man was a soldier right down to his bootheels.

Suddenly he remembered that he was supposed to keep a lookout for Indians, and he cast a quick glance behind him and on all sides, but no one was in sight. There wasn't anything to worry about now, he decided. None of the Utes would be this far north from the reservation. They'd be too near the soldiers under Lieutenant Butler Price who were guarding the supply depot.

All at once he felt cheated. Here they were close to the supply depot and he hadn't exchanged more than a dozen words with Melissa. Once they reached their destination, the Lieutenant would give her his attention, and Private Billy Buckles might as well go fishing.

"We'd best take a sashay down to the creek and water our horses," he said.

Melissa started as if she had been pulled back abruptly from the thoughts that had completely absorbed her. "We're almost there, aren't we?" she asked.

"Just about," he said, "but I noticed you didn't water your horse when we left the river. Don't seem smart to let it go when you ain't sure what's going to happen, or how we might have to use him."

"All right, Billy," she said.

They angled down the steep bank to the creek and, finding an open place in the brush, watered their horses, Billy gripping his Springfield in his right hand. After the horses had their fill, Billy lingered, his gaze on Melissa's face.

She looked at him and glanced away, embarrassed by his scrutiny. She asked, "Hadn't we better mosey along?"

"No hurry, I guess," he said. "I've been watching you, Melissa. Something's worrying you. Can I help?"

She shook her head, blinking back the tears that suddenly threatened. When she had regained control of herself, she said, "Nothing can help me, Billy, except Lee coming back. I'm scared. I guess I was never so scared in my life, not even when Pa was killed, or when I was alone in the house with Ma lying dead in her room. When I start thinking about how it would be if Lee got killed, I tighten up inside so I can't breathe. I wouldn't even want to live. And to think he's risking his life for a man like Boman and a woman like Caroline."

"You best stop worrying," he said. "Lee don't want to get killed no more'n you want him to, so he'll be careful. Besides, I guess he can do anything he sets his mind to."

For the first time since Lee had left a small smile touched the corners of Melissa's mouth. She said, "You think a lot of him, don't you?"

He looked away, hoping that she never found out about the murderous thoughts that had been in his mind earlier. He was ashamed of them, and he wished Lee didn't know. The truth was he wanted Lee's respect more than any other man's, more than Curly Joe Horn's or Amen Brown's or even Sergeant O'Brien's, but how could a man respect you when he knew that you had once thought of murdering him? Besides, Lee had not hesitated about going after Caroline and Boman, the very thing he himself had been afraid to do.

"Yeah, I think a lot of him," he said finally. "I didn't know how much until we got into the fight Monday. He's a hell of a good man, Melissa."

"Of course he is," she said. "That's why I love him. I guess it sounds ridiculous, but I felt that way the first time I saw him. I didn't know for sure he loved me until he came back from the Agency a few days ago and asked me to marry him. You see how it would be if I lost him now."

She stopped, her fists clenched, the pulse throbbing in her temples, and then she added, "You're right, Billy. I'd best stop worrying."

He dug his toe into the soft dirt at the edge of the creek.

"Yeah, that's what you'd better do." He paused, and then went on, his voice filled with emotion, "He's the lucky one to have you loving him, Melissa. I could have been lucky, too, if I'd had sense enough to know it. I left a girl once who was in love with me."

"Tell me about her."

He hesitated, wondering why he had said that to her, and wondering, too, why he had thought of Lucy at all. He said slowly, "She was a neighbor girl. I know she loved me and I know I could have married her and gone to work for her father in his store. She was pretty and good and . . . and . . ." He looked at Melissa and blurted out, "I never knew until this minute what a damned fool I was."

"How long ago was that?"

"Two years. I was only eighteen and I just didn't want to be tied down."

"You never went back to see her? Or you never even wrote to her?"

"No."

"Then you *are* a fool," Melissa said bluntly.

He saw her face suddenly tighten and go white, then he heard her scream. He whirled to see two Indians slide down the bank, the rocks that were loosened by them rattling down the steep slope. He didn't know where they came from. He only knew he had been negligent in not watching, in staying down here by the creek and giving them a chance to sneak up on him and Melissa.

In this one horrible moment time seemed to stretch on and on. He had heard men who had thought they were drowning tell about how their past lives had rushed through their minds in a second or two. It was that way with him now. He wished he could live some of it over, but he and Melissa would die, trapped here beside the creek by his own carelessness.

He saw their evil painted faces; he saw the cocked rifles in their hands that were being raised to fire, and the thought burned across his mind like a scorching fire that he was still little Billy Buckles who never got anywhere in time and never did anything right.

Without realizing that he had raised his Springfield, he heard it roar, felt it smashed against his shoulder and saw the great cloud of smoke. He had fired by instinct, and was surprised to see the first Ute fall and roll over and over into the creek.

They had fired too, and missed, and now he rushed at the second warrior, who was partially hidden by the whirling smoke. Nothing was really clear, but he had a vague hope that he might be able to club the man to death with his carbine. For a moment he thought maybe it was all a nightmare; maybe when he swung the Springfield he wouldn't hit anything, because there was no Indian in front of him.

But when the Ute fired a second time and the bullet struck Billy and he was falling backward and pinwheeling into space, he knew this was real. He had the impression that his left shoulder had been blown away from the rest of his body. The ground hit him and he thought he heard shooting, and then the blessed blackness reached up and drew him into its embrace.

Melissa stared at the second Indian, who had fallen a few feet in front of her. She had killed him. Her right hand hung at her side still gripping her revolver, smoke making a shifting pattern as it left the muzzle. She had triggered off two shots, the first a clean miss, the second a perfect hit, the slug smashing into the Indian's face and ripping upward through his brain.

Her gaze swept the bank, but there weren't any more of them. For a moment she was afraid she was going to faint. Her knees seemed about to give way, but she refused to let them. She was alive, she was not injured, and most of all, she was not Caroline. She was her mother's daughter and she knew exactly what her mother would have done.

Kneeling beside Billy, she saw that the bullet had driven into his chest on the left side, but it was high. He was still alive, his pulse was good, and if she could stop the bleeding she thought he might pull through. She tore off the bottom of her petticoat and, wadding it up into a ball, slipped it between his undershirt and the wound.

Somehow she got him off the ground and across his saddle. She tied him there, trying so hard to hurry that her fingers seemed to be all thumbs. Maybe she was doing the wrong thing. He might die before she reached the supply depot, but she didn't know anything else to do. Mounting her buckskin, she led Billy's horse up the bank and turned north.

Chapter 22

LEE HAD not followed Nevero's trail long before he decided that the Utes were heading toward a definite place somewhere in the timber southeast of the Simms-Boman trading post. He thought at first they intended to swing east, and then travel south toward White River, but after noting that they held the same general direction mile after mile, he wasn't sure.

He did not know, either, why two of the five Indians had separated from the three he was following. By mid-afternoon he had the idea that Nevero was going as far back into the high country as he could, wanting nothing to do with Jack and Colorow and the other chiefs and subchiefs who were leading the attack on the trapped soldiers and civilians on Milk Creek. They had made little attempt to hide their tracks, apparently confident that no one would follow them.

Once, in his haste, Lee lost the track and had to go back and pick it up, but most of the time he had no trouble, because Nevero was picking the easiest route he could, following canyons if their direction was right; or, if he left them, he was angling up the south sides and keeping to the ridge a mile or two before making another turn to the south.

His route was far from a straight line, but the general direction could not be mistaken. If he kept going, he would eventually reach the Flattops near the head of White River, but this didn't seem reasonable. It would be cold up there even in early fall, with snow probably on the ground.

Lee had just topped a ridge when he heard what sounded like a man's scream. He pulled up and listened, not quite sure what he had heard. Then it came again, long and high, the kind of sound that never would leave a man's throat unless the pain was so excruciating that he had lost all self-control. Nevero had made camp, Lee decided, and Lucky Boman's luck had run out at last.

A shallow valley lay to Lee's right, the small twisting

stream at the bottom shaded by aspens. Most of the leaves had fallen, and the ones that remained had turned to gold, but there were so few that the trees had a half-naked look, and furnished little if any cover.

When Lee swung to his right and could look down into the valley, he saw Nevero's camp a short distance upstream. They had a small fire going. Nevero, still wearing his derby, was talking to Caroline, who lay on the ground near the fire, her hands and feet tied. Boman was a bloody figure on the ground not far away, as shapeless as a bundle of rags. He would never scream again. In a way he had been lucky, for the Indians could have made the torture last a great deal longer than they had.

Lee moved back and tied his horse, then lifted the Winchester from the scabbard and moved silently along the ridge top until he was directly opposite the Indian camp. He dropped belly-flat and wormed his way to the edge. He lay there in the brush for a time, staring at the three Utes and Caroline.

It occurred to him that this was as far as Nevero intended to go. Perhaps he planned to wait for the two absent Indians, then cut south toward White River. If he had left Milk Creek about the time the fight had started, or before, he would not know what had happened.

It seemed reasonable that Jack had sent Nevero and the others north on a scouting trip to see if Thornburgh had left part of his force somewhere to the north, which might reinforce him later on. That could be the reason two of the Utes were missing. Picking up Caroline and Boman would be Nevero's idea. Jack would not care what happened to Boman, and he might not be much concerned about Caroline's fate, but he would very likely be furious if he knew Nevero had wasted so much time because he had been fascinated by a white woman. If Nevero thought of this, as he probably would, it seemed to Lee that he would leave her body here, where it was unlikely it would ever be found, and would give Jack some other explanation of the delay.

Lee slipped downslope through the brush, moving slowly and silently. Nevero was still talking to Caroline. The other two Utes were young warriors, probably not over twenty. They stood motionless, watching Nevero and Caroline, their rifles in their hands. Lee, who had almost reached the bottom now, thought that if he had any chance to take the three of them, he would have to do it while they were grouped close together.

The two missing Indians bothered Lee more than anything. else. If Nevero had stopped here to wait for them and they moved in behind Lee, he was dead and so was Caroline. He'd start the action now, he decided, and get Caroline out of here as fast as he could.

He eased forward to the last clump of brush that was big enough to hide him, and had started to raise his Winchester when Nevero bent over Caroline with a knife and cut the thongs that bound her hands and ankles. Lee hesitated, easing the pressure of his trigger finger. At that exact moment Nevero moved between him and the girl, and he could not risk a shot.

A moment later Caroline was on her feet and backing away from Nevero, her face so distorted by fear it was hardly recognizable. Nevero motioned toward the horses as he said something to the other Indians, probably wanting them to go somewhere else. They turned just as Lee moved away from the brush toward a tall boulder and caught Nevero in his sights. Before he could squeeze off the shot, his right foot slipped, rolling a small twig forward. It broke under his weight, cracking with a sound that seemed as loud as thunder in the afternoon stillness.

The three Utes whirled toward him, Nevero lunging for his Henry rifle that was on the ground. The other two fired as Lee swung his Winchester from Nevero to the one nearest him and squeezed off a shot. The slug caught the Indian in the mouth, killing him instantly and making his shot go wild.

The second Ute's shot hit the boulder beside Lee, the rock splinters stinging his face. Lee missed his next shot and knew at once it might prove fatal, for Nevero had his rifle in his hands and was turning to Caroline, who had started to run.

Lee's third shot struck Nevero in the neck and knocked him to the ground. He was using up seconds that gave the remaining Indian time to aim, and Lee was in the open, an easy target for the Ute. He spilled forward to the ground, moving as fast as he could, though it seemed to him he was unable to move with any speed at all. The Indian's rifle spurted fire, the bullet slapping through the crown of Lee's hat.

107

Lee levered another shot into place and fired, tilting the Winchester so that the bullet caught the Ute under the chin and angled upward through his head. An instant later Lee was on his feet, calling, "Caroline."

She had started to run up the creek, screaming hysterically. He yelled again, "Caroline," and ran after her. She heard him this time and turned. When she saw him she stopped, lurched forward one step, and then toppled to the ground in a faint.

He let her lie there while he made sure the Indians were dead, then he jammed new loads into the magazine, still thinking of the two missing Indians. If they were close enough to hear the shooting, they'd be here any moment. He picked Caroline up and ran toward the horses.

She came to a few seconds later and screamed, "Put me down. Put me down." He stopped, staring at her and thinking she was still hysterical, but her eyes looked normal enough. So did her voice when she said, "God damn it, Lee, put me down."

He let go. She fell hard, hitting on her seat, then flattened out so that her head and heels struck the ground simultaneously. He ran on to the horses, released the Indian ponies, pulled the saddle off the horse Boman had ridden and let him go. He untied Caroline's horse and led him back to the girl, who was bending over Boman's body. She rose just as Lee came with the horse, the heavy money belt in her hand.

She stared at Lee, and said defensively, "Can you think of anyone who has a better claim to this money than I have?"

"You're not crying much over your man getting killed," Lee said.

"*My man,*" she said bitterly. "After they caught us he told me what he had planned to do with me. He never loved me, Lee. He was just going to use me after we got to Denver."

"Take the money," Lee said curtly, and motioned to the saddle. "Climb on. My horse is on top of the ridge."

He gave her a hand and turned and started up the slope, Caroline following on her horse. He said nothing until he reached the top and mounted, then he asked, "Did you know that Boman murdered your mother?"

For a moment he thought she was going to faint again and fall out of her saddle, but she gripped the horn and hung on as she stared at him, her lips parted. She was dirty, her clothes were rumpled, and her hair was disheveled. She was as heartless as any woman he had ever known, he thought, judging from the way she had gone after Boman's money belt, and he wondered why he had ever thought he loved her. If she felt any grief because of Boman's painful death, she didn't show it, but perhaps she had learned to hate him in the last hours of their lives together. Now, for the first time, she seemed genuinely shocked.

"I don't believe it," she said.

"I didn't see the shooting," he told her, "but I helped bury your ma. Melissa said he came after your things Tuesday morning and your ma wouldn't let him have them. Melissa was outside. She heard a shot and ran into the house and found your ma lying on the floor, a rifle beside her. Boman was pulling out."

"The bastard," she said. "The lying bastard. She ran him off with a shotgun, he told me, and that's why he didn't get my clothes." She shut her eyes and swayed in the saddle, then she said, "Go on, Lee. I'll keep up."

They rode until after sundown and stopped when Caroline insisted she could not go any farther. They camped beside the Bear, Lee making a small fire to cook supper, and afterward put it out in spite of Caroline's protests.

"We'll stay here until you think you're rested enough to travel," he said. "I don't know how many Indians are riding around looking for any stray whites they can find, but there were five, including Nevero, and only three had you, so there are at least two more around here somewhere."

She was quiet for a long time. The darkness pressed down around them so that he could not see her clearly. Presently she moved to him and leaned against him, shivering. She said, "Hold me, Lee. Hold me hard and keep me warm. I'm cold and I'm scared, and I . . . I guess I feel guilty about Ma's death."

"You'd better lie down," he said. "I'll throw my saddle blanket over you."

She shivered again, and still pressed against him. She whispered, "Don't hate me, Lee. You're all I've got left. I never knew how brave you were until today. I know you still love me, or you wouldn't have come after me."

He put a hand against her and shoved her away from him. He said, "I don't love you, and you're not worth hating.

You've got Boman's money belt, so I guess you'll make out pretty good. Now don't bother me any more."

She didn't. They were on the move with the first light of dawn. She did not say a word to him all the way north to the supply depot.

Chapter 23

LEE AND Caroline reached the supply depot shortly before noon Friday. Melissa ran to meet them as soon as she saw them. Lee swung down from the saddle and opened his arms to her. A moment later she was in them, and she was saying over and over, "I was afraid for you, Lee. I was so afraid."

He pushed her back and looked at her hungrily for a moment. He said, "You're here and you're safe, and I'm here and I'm safe, and I guess that's all that counts." He pulled her to him again and she nestled against him, wanting the safety of his strong arms around her. As he held her, he realized how great his love was for her, more than he had known, because he understood now for the first time how incomplete his life would be without her.

Presently she drew away from him and looked up into his face. She asked, "Is this the way our married life is going to be, you riding off into danger time after time?"

"No," he said. "I'm done riding. Alone, I mean. Our next ride will be to Rawlins, where we'll get married."

Caroline spoke for the first time. "Well," she said, "aren't you glad to see me, Melissa?"

Slowly Melissa turned toward her sister. Lee had wondered how this greeting would go, and for a moment he thought Melissa would say no, that she had hoped the Indians would give Caroline exactly what she deserved, but she didn't say it. She answered without any show of emotion, "Of course I'm glad to see you."

Melissa embraced her, and suddenly Caroline began to cry. She whispered, "I didn't know about Ma, 'Lissa. Before God, I never dreamed he'd do what he did."

Melissa began to cry, too. They walked off together, Melissa's arm around Caroline. Lee, watching them, told himself that Caroline could never be believed. She was a greedy bitch, a liar and a phony, and he wondered if she was taking Melissa in—Melissa, who had known her for what she was long before Lee had.

Then, for some reason that he could not identify, the thought struck him that perhaps this time she wasn't acting out a role. It was possible that for once she was being honest. He wondered if she would turn to Melissa to be protected and looked out for. She would find in her sister the same strength she had found in her mother.

He dismissed this line of thinking as being preposterous. Melissa had no reason to love Caroline, and she would not forget the bitter years when she had worked like a man while Caroline had been pampered like a sick child.

He found Lieutenant Butler Price and made his report. "None of the Indians have been this far north," the Lieutenant said thoughtfully, "except the two that Buckles and Miss Frazer ran into a little ways south of here. I still don't know why—"

"Two?" Lee interrupted, and gripped the Lieutenant's arm. "You say Buckles and Melissa ran into two of them?"

"They did, and damned near got killed," Price said. "Buckles has a bullet hole in his chest. He's still alive, but we've got to get him to a hospital. Miss Frazer didn't tell you?"

"No, she didn't."

Price told him what had happened, and added, "The way Miss Frazer tells it, Buckles should have a medal for bravery. He shot one of them and was running at the other one aiming to club him down when the Ute let him have it point-blank. If the girl hadn't had a revolver and hadn't kept her head and hadn't been a good shot, they'd both have been killed."

Lee rubbed his face with both hands. He was tired and hungry, and now he was sour-tempered. "I thought I had to go after Melissa's sister and Boman," he said, "and I couldn't risk taking Melissa. I never figured any of the Indians would get this far north of the Bear. Rankin said the same. Damn it, I should have had them stay at the Frazer house till I got back."

Price shook his head. "No, you did the right thing. It was something none of us could have foreseen." He hesitated, and then continued, "I don't want to reprimand Buckles, because he showed a lot of courage in doing what he did. I realize he's young and he hadn't been in the Army very long, but damn it, he should have kept his eyes open, and he shouldn't have stayed down there on the creek where the Indians had a chance to slip up on them."

Lee thought about it a minute. "No, I don't think he should be reprimanded," he said. "What he needs more than anything is a little bragging. Give him time to finish growing up, Lieutenant, and he'll make a good soldier."

"That's what Miss Frazer told me," Price said, smiling slightly. "All right, we'll brag on him and let it go at that." He nodded toward one of the tents. "He's in there, but I wouldn't talk to him much. He's feverish and the wound's hurting him like hell."

"I'll see him just a minute and then I want something to eat," Lee said. "After that I'm going down to the creek where it's quiet and sleep. I don't remember when I ate last, and I've slept damned little lately. I feel like a walking dead man."

"You even look a little bit like a walking dead man," Price said. "We'll feed you, and if anybody disturbs your nap, I'll court-martial him."

"If it's all right, I'll take the Frazer girls to Rawlins in the morning," Lee said. "Melissa and me are getting married, and Caroline will be leaving on the train."

Price hesitated, studying Lee a moment. Then he said, "Starbuck, I expect a relief party here any time. Tomorrow or Sunday at the latest. Rankin and Moquin went through here on their way north. Buckles rode with Moquin for a while, so I'm sure he was past any Indians who might have come this far north."

Lee knew what was coming. He was too tired and hungry to stand here talking, so he waited a moment until his temper was under control and then merely said, "Well?"

"I don't know who will command the relief expedition," Price said, "but it will probably be Colonel Wesley Merritt. He may want you to guide him to the battlefield."

"He can go to hell," Lee said, and swung around and walked away.

He stepped into the tent. Billy was lying on a cot, his sharp-featured face bright with fever, but he recognized Lee. He said hoarsely, "I was a fool. I almost let Melissa get killed."

"But the fact is you didn't," Lee said. "I was just talking

112

to the Lieutenant. He said you should get a medal for bravery. We're proud of you, boy."

Billy closed his eyes and ran the tip of his tongue over his cracked lips. "Melissa was just making it sound good, but we made it, and I guess that's what counts. I'm glad you did, too. Melissa was worried about you."

"You try to sleep," Lee said. "I'll stop in later."

He left, and as soon as he had eaten his dinner he slipped away and slept until evening. When he returned to the camp, he found Melissa sitting beside Billy's cot, a damp cloth in her hand. She glanced at Lee and shook her head.

"His fever's worse," she said. "He's got to have a doctor."

"There'll be one with the relief party," Lee said. "Where's Caroline?"

"Asleep in a tent." She reached up and took Lee's hand. "Honey, do you have any idea how much Billy worships you?"

Lee smiled, remembering that not very long ago the boy had thought seriously of murdering him. He said, "No, but I know he's in love with you."

"Not any more," she said. "I never really knew him until you left us together, but he talked about himself a little today. He's not had an easy life and he's made some mistakes. When he left home there was a neighbor girl who loved him. He never wrote to her and never went back to see her. Well, I'm going to write to her and tell her what a brave man he is, and maybe she'll write to him."

"And maybe by this time she's married and has twins," he said. "You'd better think about the responsibility that Cupid has before you start playing that you're him."

"I know," she said quickly. "I just thought I'd write and find out. If she loved him as much as he thinks she did, she'll be waiting for him." She saw by Lee's expression that he did not believe any girl would wait two years without hearing from a man. She said defensively, "It won't hurt to write to her, will it?"

"No," he said. "You go ahead, 'Lissa."

"I'm happy," she said. "I just want Billy and his Lucy to be as happy as I am."

He bent and kissed her, then he said, "I'll eat supper and go to sleep again. I don't think I'll ever catch up."

He left the tent, wondering if he should have told her he might be riding into danger again. After his spell of surliness

113

at noon he had changed his mind. When he saw Lieutenant Price he told him that he had.

"I don't want to go," he said, "but I will if the commander of the relief party wants me to guide him. I know what it's like down there. By this time they're about out of grub, and some of the wounded will have died. The dead horses and mules will be stinking like hell. I'd be ashamed of myself the rest of my life if I didn't go, because I can save them a little time."

Price held out his hand. "I thought you would, Starbuck. All you needed was a little sleep."

Lee was still asleep the next day when the relief party arrived, four companies of cavalry and one hundred fifty infantrymen in wagons. The commander was Colonel Wesley Merritt, as Price had guessed. He conferred briefly with the Lieutenant, who told him what had happened, then he sent for Lee.

He shook hands with Lee, his sharp eyes making a quick appraisal. He said, "Certainly I want you to guide us. Time is of the essence. I have only faint hopes of saving the lives of Meeker and his people, but I do believe we can save what is left of Major Thornburgh's expedition. I understand the Major was killed at the beginning of the fight."

"That was what Captain Payne was afraid of," Lee said, "although we did not find the body."

"You'll move south with us, Lieutenant," Merritt said, turning to Price. "We may need all the men we can raise if the Uncompahgres and the southern Utes join the hostiles."

"They won't," Lee said.

Merritt whirled to face him. "Mr. Starbuck, you may know this country, but I will not accept you as an expert on Indian behavior."

"There are two women in camp and a wounded soldier," Lee shot back. "You have no business taking them south into Ute country."

"I have no such intentions," Merritt said. "A surgeon is with the wounded man now. I will send him north in a wagon with a detail, and the women will go with them."

"Good," Lee said.

He found Melissa in Billy's tent and drew her outside. "What does the doctor say?"

"It's a long ways to the post hospital," she said, "and the jolting in the wagon may open the wound and start it bleeding, but the doctor thinks he will be all right."

114

"Honey, I've got to go again," he said. "They want me to guide them, and there isn't anyone else."

He expected her to argue, but she didn't. She kissed him tenderly, and she said, "I'll wait for you in Rawlins. We know we can find a preacher there."

"I'll see you in a few days," he said. "You tell that preacher to be ready to say 'I pronounce you man and wife.' "

She laughed. "I'll have him practicing every day until you get there."

A short time later the long column rolled south, Lee riding in front alongside Colonel Merritt. He wondered if this was to be another ride into danger; or had the Utes quit fighting and withdrawn into the mountains to the south? They wouldn't withdraw if anyone was still alive inside the wagon circle, he thought; and that, he decided dismally, was the answer to his question.

Chapter 24

JOE RANKIN had brought word of the battle to Rawlins and had immediately put the news on the wire, Colonel Merritt told Lee. A fabulous ride, the officer said, 170 miles in 28 hours. It would go down in history, he opined, along with other great rides, rides that were too fantastic to be believed when they were recorded for later generations to be read about, but this one had really happened.

Within two hours and a half from the time Joe Rankin had brought his tired horse into Rawlins, Colonel Merritt had started throwing a relief party together at Fort D.A. Russell. Years from now, he said, Joe Rankin would become a legend, a legend that would grow with the telling.

Lee stared ahead at the dusty road that had been carved through the sagebrush by wheels and hoofs, and he thought of the opinion that Billy Buckles and some of the others had held of Joe Rankin. They had been wrong, for when the blue chips were all down the man had come through, for all of his loud talk and white buckskins. Colonel Merritt had probably been right. Time would make a legend out of Joe Rankin, and the legend would grow with the telling.

Now that they were close to the battle scene, Merritt would not stop. They made seventy miles, traveling night and day, and it was near dawn Sunday morning when the column halted. They were close enough to the location of Payne's command to hear firing if there was any, but no sound came to them.

"What do you think, Starbuck?" Merritt asked.

"It's hard to tell," Lee answered. "Jack may have pulled his men off; but if he hasn't, we'll be in a hell of a shape as soon as it gets daylight."

"I'm not worried about that as much as I am that we've got here too late," Merritt said. "I don't want to take a risk of running into an ambush if they're all dead, but if some of them are alive we'll take any risk to save them."

He ordered the bugler to sound Officers' Call. Lee listened as the sharp sound broke out of the instrument and was flung back by the mountains in echo. Silence then for what must have been only seconds, but to Lee and Merritt and the others behind them in the column it seemed an eternity until they heard an answering bugle call, muted by distance.

"Thank God!" Merritt said. "If the bugler's alive, some of the rest must be, too."

They moved on in the growing light, and a little later came in sight of the breastworks. The garrison poured over dead horses and mules and through openings between the wagons, yelling and waving their hats. Some were wounded, and many who were not injured were sick, and all were hungry. They were jubilant, too, forgetting for a moment all the danger and suffering in the joy of deliverance. They had not really expected it, Lee thought, and had made up their minds to die here in the dirt and stink where they had been forted up for six days.

Amen Brown was the first to reach Lee. He shook his hand, looking taller and thinner than ever. He said, "By God, I never heard a welcomer sound than that bugle, or a welcomer sight than you boys riding up. Did Billy get through?"

"He sure did," Lee said, "and then he ran into a couple of stray Indians later and got a slug in his chest, but he's on his way to the post hospital. The doc thinks he'll make it."

"I hope he does," Brown said.

"Where's Curly Joe?"

"Dead," Brown said bitterly. "I'm to blame. I guess I'm to blame for about everything that's happened. I fired the shot that started the whole shebang, and after that I kind o' went out of my head for about twenty-four hours; but it seems like I was asking for water and Curly Joe went to the creek to get me some. A big Ute who was waiting down there cut him wide open with a knife. Joe blowed his head off, but that don't bring Joe back."

"I'm sorry," Lee said. "He was a good man."

"A hell of a good man," Brown said, "and I'm to blame, I tell you."

"No," Lee said, "you're not to blame. Nobody's to blame. It's part of the pattern. I think Joe knew that. He knew a lot, seemed like."

"He sure did," Brown said, and turned away.

Lee, looking at him, knew that no amount of assurance would ever lift the burden of guilt from Amen Brown's conscience.

Merritt began giving orders immediately. The dead soldiers were buried, a new camp was made upstream from the breastworks to escape the sickening stench of the dead horses and mules, and the wounded were given all possible care. Major Thornburgh's body was found and brought in. Within a few hours it would be on its way north to Fort Steele.

Merritt sent Lee to scout the immediate area to the south, and when he returned near noon with word that no Indians were there, the Colonel rode out of camp with Lee and Lieutenant Cherry to examine the battlefield. After the Colonel left to go back to camp, Lee asked Cherry about Captain Dodge and his colored cavalrymen.

"It was the damnedest thing," the Lieutenant said. "Captain Dodge rode in with his Company D about sunrise Thursday. I guess they'd been moving like hell to get here. The Utes didn't see them until it was too late to turn them back. I can tell you they were welcome. There weren't enough of them to raise the siege, but they were a big help to our morale." He laughed. "Starbuck, you should have seen Captain Dodge. He was as proud of them as if they'd captured Jack himself."

Lee remembered his talk with Captain Dodge in Hayden. His desire to demonstrate that his colored troopers were as good as white soldiers had been a personal issue with him. They had joined the garrison to die or be rescued by a relief party, and so Captain Dodge had proved his point.

Lee was still thinking about it when a band of Utes suddenly came into view on the ridge above them. A moment later a white man broke over the crest and rode down the slope. He was Joe Brady from the Los Piños Agency on the Uncompahgre. He had two messages, one from the agent at Los Piños saying that Ouray was ordering the fighting to stop, and the second from Ouray giving the order.

"Jack has agreed to obey Ouray," Brady said. "He wants peace as bad as anyone."

Lee and Lieutenant Cherry took Brady back to camp. Merritt read the messages and talked to Brady. Jack had not told him exactly what had happened, but he had said in a roundabout way that Meeker and the other men at the Agency were dead and that the women and children were captives somewhere in the mountains to the south.

Merritt was furious, because he wanted to punish the Utes, or at least demonstrate that the United States Army was taking over to unscramble the mistakes that had been piled up for years, but he was held back by the precarious position of the white women and children who were captives. Brady returned to the Indians on the ridge and they disappeared toward the south.

Merritt still would not permit Lee to leave for Rawlins, insisting that there was a threat of trouble until the women and children were rescued. Lee wrote to Melissa, trying to explain to her why he could not go to her yet, and then gave it up. He said simply that Merritt still needed him and he loved her and would come to her at Rawlins as soon as possible.

The letter went north with Payne's command, which was accompanied by Captain Dodge's Company D. Merritt remained on Milk Creek until he was reinforced by Colonel C.C. Gilbert out of Fort Snelling, then he moved through Coal Creek Canyon to what was left of the Agency.

Lee looked at a scene he would never forget. Most of the buildings had been burned, and the tools and machinery in which Meeker had taken so much pride had been destroyed. The bodies of the Agency employees were scattered among the ruins. Some distance from the others Lee found Meeker's naked body. He had been shot in the head, a logging chain was fastened around his neck, and a barrel stave had been driven down his throat.

Lee walked away, sick. He understood the symbolism of

the chain, for he knew how much Jack and his people had feared being put in chains and dragged off by force to Indian Territory or Florida. He could not explain it to either Colonel Merritt or Colonel Snelling, so he did not try, but he was remembering the last night he'd been here and the good supper Arvilla Meeker had cooked, and his talk with Nathan Meeker that evening.

Lee had told Meeker he wouldn't be alive to need protection by the time the soldiers arrived. He remembered saying it as clearly as if his talk with the agent had been no more than an hour ago. His words had made him a better prophet than he had dreamed.

In his way, he told himself, he had second sight just as Curly Joe Horn had had, the second sight of a man who had watched the inexorable trend of events and knew what was inevitable unless the trend was changed. But it had not been changed, and so Nathan Meeker, a good man, an honest man, a dreamer with a vision of a great future for the Utes, had been rewarded with a terrible death, along with every white man at the Agency.

Merritt did not let Lee go until he received news that the women and children had been rescued, then he shook hands with Lee and thanked him and wished him good luck. Lee rode north at once, up Coal Creek Canyon and over Yellow Jacket Pass and past the battlefield.

For some reason he could not put Curly Joe Horn out of his mind. He had the weird feeling that the man was talking to him in his gentle way. He had no idea what Curly Joe was saying, but it didn't seem to be important. The important thing was that he had known Curly Joe, a soldier who had sought death and had found it, and then Lee wondered if at that last fatal moment he had really wanted to die. This was something he would never know, and still he pondered it until he was beyond Williams Fork.

He reached Rawlins early in the afternoon on a cold, windy day in late October. He found Melissa in her hotel room and told her to go prime the preacher, that they'd be married as soon as he had a bath, a shave, and a haircut, and could buy a new suit. She kissed him, ran her hands over his arms and shoulders, and cried a little, and he understood without her telling him how hard these waiting days had been for her.

"All right, I'll go prime the preacher." She raised her hands to his face and felt of his beard and blinked away the tears, and then she said, half laughing and half crying, "Oh, honey, I don't think you're Lee Starbuck. I think you're a bear and you've come to carry me off to a cave."

He almost said he was going to carry her home to a boar's nest, but he was afraid it would bring up the subject of Caroline. She had been a nagging worry in the back of his mind from the day he had ridden south with the relief party. He said simply, "Sure I'm a bear. I'll be back growling at you in a little while."

He did not even ask her about Billy Buckles until after the ceremony and they were in her room with a bottle of champagne cooling on the bureau. He asked, "Have you seen or heard of Billy lately?"

She nodded. "I went out to Fort Steele yesterday. He's coming along fine."

"How did your playing Cupid work out?"

Embarrassed, she said, "He hasn't heard from Lucy yet, but he will. You'll see."

He jammed his hands into his pockets and walked to the window and stood staring into the darkness. He wasn't sure why it was so hard to ask about Caroline, except that she was Melissa's only living relative, and so their parting might have been more difficult than either girl had foreseen.

"Has Caroline left yet?" he asked finally.

"Three days ago." Melissa crossed the room to him and put her arm in his. "Lee, it was the strangest thing. She didn't want to go. After all she's said about hating Bear Valley, she asked if she could go back and live in your cabin with us. I told her it wouldn't do, and reminded her that she used to call it a boar's nest. She started to cry and said she wished she had the last two years to live over. She said your cabin looked like a palace to her now."

This was exactly what he had thought Caroline would say, and he had been afraid that Melissa would weaken and feel so sorry for her that she would agree to some arrangement that wouldn't work. Now he remained silent, sensing that she had something more to say.

Melissa took a long breath, and then went on, "Lee, you know how I used to hate Caroline. She would be in the house sewing or knitting or taking a nap while I was out working in the cold. She was seeing Boman all the time and lying to Ma and nagging her about leaving Bear Valley and going to Denver.

120

"The strangest part of the whole business is that I don't hate her any more. I feel sorry for her, because even with Boman's money she's going to be miserable all her life. She needs someone to look out for her like Ma did and the way she thought Boman was going to. Now she doesn't have anyone. She's afraid, Lee. She's terribly afraid, and here I am, with everything."

"Not quite everything," he said.

"Well, everything that counts."

Pleased, he laughed aloud. "Let's drink a toast, 'Lissa. To the Lee Starbucks: May all their troubles be little ones. It's been said before, but I don't believe it's ever meant as much as it does to us."

"And many of them," she added. "Fill the glasses, Lee. Of course I'll drink to that."

Wayne D. Overholser has won three Golden Spur awards from the Western Writers of America and has a long list of fine Western titles to his credit. He was born in Pomeroy, Washington, and attended the University of Montana, University of Oregon, and the University of Southern California before becoming a public school teacher and principal in various Oregon communities. He began writing for Western pulp magazines in 1936 and within a couple of years was a regular contributor to Street & Smith's *Western Story* and Fiction House's *Lariat Story Magazine*. *Buckaroo's Code* (1948) was his first Western novel and remains one of his best. In the 1950s and 1960s, having retired from academic work to concentrate on writing, he would publish as many as four books a year under his own name or a pseudonym, most prominently as Joseph Wayne. *The Bitter Night*, *The Lone Deputy*, and *The Violent Land* are among the finest of the early Overholser titles. He was asked by William MacLeod Raine, that dean among Western writers, to complete his last novel after Raine's death. Some of Overholser's most rewarding novels were actually collaborations with other Western writers: *Colorado Gold* with Chad Merriman and *Showdown at Stony Creek* with Lewis B. Patten. Overholser's Western novels, no matter under what name they have been published, are based on a solid knowledge of the history and customs of the American frontier West, particularly when set in his two favorite Western states, Oregon and Colorado. When it comes to his characters, he writes with skill, an uncommon sensitivity, and a consistently vivid and accurate vision of a way of life unique in human history.